Albin's Letters

A NOVELLA BY
ROSIE ATKINSON

To Irene & Bud,

Thank you for reading my first book!

Love,

Rosie Atkinson

ALBIN'S LETTERS

For my mother
Esteri (Esther) Putkonen Bruder Brown
April 9, 1907 — May 12, 2007

ALBIN'S LETTERS

Chapter 1

August 27, 1905

Hilda stood on the deck as the steamship, St. Paul, approached Ellis Island. The sun had just set over the city of New York and lights were beginning to twinkle on like fireflies spread across the land above the harbor.

Warm air came in waves from the still-hot uplands and Hilda used her lace-edged handkerchief to dab the perspiration from her forehead and neck. She wished she could remove the high top lace-up boots that made her feet ache. Hilda was sure the boots were designed to cover her ankles lest a pair of wandering male eyes might have a glimpse of her shapely legs. Her brother, it seemed to Hilda, was the cause of all of her pain in recent months. She knew John did not invent these cumbersome, long, heavy skirts and petticoats which were the fashion of the day, but she was sure he was behind the push to make all young women in Finland wear them in public. Most of all she hated the tight corset she was forced to wear under it all.

Everything had been too confusing before

she made the decision to leave her homeland for America to find Albin, her childhood sweetheart now living somewhere in this foreign place called America. She had been in the midst of planning a wedding and she had never told her Swedish fiancé that it was Albin whom she truly loved, but whom she believed had forgotten her in the years since he left Finland. He had vowed to stay in touch with Hilda and she believed he had broken that promise. Her world turned upside down when her brother confessed to having kept Albin's letters from her until the day before her wedding to Sven was to take place.

As she stood at the rail of the ship a wave of nausea came over her. No one was around to see her throw up over the side.

Most of the passengers had retired to their staterooms after the captain had announced they would remain at anchor until dawn because the dock was closed and the Ellis Island work force, including the U.S. Customs officers, had gone home for the night. Hilda and a few of the others were too restless to go to bed having spent five days on the ocean rocking and rolling with the undulating sea. They were so close to realizing a dream.

For some of these emigrants, a new start in a different country may have been the solution to a perceived problem. For others, it may have been trading one kind of misery for another. Hilda used to listen to her brother when he told her to be careful what she wished for. She had always had high hopes and believed something good was about to happen when she least expected it. Her experiences in life so far proved that this wasn't always the case.

It had been so long since Hilda had seen Albin. She wondered how much he might have changed since he left Finland. Her country now seemed so far away as the ship approached this new land. The butterflies in her stomach told her she was about to experience life as she'd never known it before. She couldn't explain the tears that now streamed down her cheeks. Were they tears of joy in anticipation of seeing her sweetheart again after all these years? Or were they tears of regret for leaving all that had been familiar to her for the past 22 years?

Hilda thought back to the first time she met Albin. It was a hot night…

Albin Putkonen had just finished sanding down
the last of fourteen cabinet doors his boss had set
out for him to do that day. It was hot in the little
shop in Arvo Makela's big old barn in back of the
main house. Albin wiped the sweat from his brow
with his already damp handkerchief when Mr.
Makela said, "You have worked hard today, Albin,
and it's hot. Go home and get some rest. You can
finish sanding in the morning".

Working for Arvo Makela wasn't as physically
taxing as other jobs Albin could have chosen to earn
a living. He had tried making copper pots to make
money and it was satisfying but more a hobby than
a job. He was tired today so he was more than happy
to do as the boss said. His work shirt was soaked
with sweat and the sawdust was sticking to his
clothing and hair. Getting out of the hot, dusty barn
was a welcome order.

Albin had been working for Makela about four
months now, ever since he left Mikkeli to find work
in Finland's capital city. Good jobs were hard to find
anywhere in Finland. Most of his friends believed
it was because the Russians had taken over their
country. Working conditions weren't any better here
than they were in Mikkeli. Cabinetry wasn't what
Albin saw himself doing for the rest of his life, but it

was honest work and he needed to support himself somehow.

Makela had advertised for a finish carpenter in the paper and Albin answered the ad even if he didn't know what kind of work it really was.

When Albin went to apply for the job, Makela took one look at him and decided he didn't look strong enough to handle the heavy lumber and woodworking tools. Albin's looks were deceiving. He had stopped growing taller than four-feet-ten when he was about 14 years old and he was often mistaken for a boy. Most of his brothers and sisters were taller but this never seemed to bother him. When he was in school he took up sports. Wrestling became his favorite. Albin developed an enviable physique after only a few months of working out in the gym.

The only problem with being short was he could never find a girlfriend who didn't tower over him. Despite this one drawback Albin was never self conscious about his height.

Makela was a giant at six feet when he stood next to Albin. He wasn't that much older, but he treated Albin like a son. He was kind and patient as Albin apprenticed for him and learned the woodworking trade quickly. Makela liked the fact that Albin remembered everything he taught him and that he seldom had to repeat instructions.

The two often talked about politics when they worked together in the little shop. Albin liked to hear what people were thinking, and about what the Russians were doing to his country. Makela was very opinionated and Albin appreciated getting feedback on these matters. Albin memorized his boss's remarks so he could repeat them verbatim to his young friends.

At the end of the century and the beginning of the 1900s, Finland was going through some serious changes with many Russian families moving into their neighborhoods. The latest rumor was that all young men would have to serve in the Russian army. Albin and his friends were worried that any day now they would be hauled off to army training camps in Siberia.

Many of Albin's old classmates had already left the country and sailed to America to find a better life. He wondered how long it would be before he, too, would pack up to leave all that was familiar to him. America was where many of his countrymen had already gone. There had been many articles in the newspapers about America. Also, letters from neighbors who had sailed the Atlantic to find their fortune in the new country told of magnificent living conditions. They wrote of beautiful forests and gleaming big cities where they could live out their lives in luxury. He couldn't tell how much of this was true. What he read sounded like fiction. But, if it were true, he wondered why Makela and his friends hadn't left Finland years ago for a future in America.

Some of the photographs circulating in those days were of a World's Fair in Chicago that depicted a gleaming city, just the opposite of the real Chicago that was smudged with dirty coal dust and smoke from factory chimneys.

Makela had mentioned to Albin on the second day he worked for him that he had thought about leaving Finland but his wife was too afraid of the unknown. She wasn't so quick to accept the stories about streets paved with gold. She loved her family and her home and didn't think politics and promises of Utopia should drive them out of their country. Besides, Makela and Helga had four children and it was well known that men with children and a wife to support would not be drafted into the military.

Albin rode his bicycle two miles through the back alleys of Helsinki to his apartment building, a three-story drab concrete structure with the tiniest of windows. It was still light enough so he could easily find his way home. He could think of nothing else but seeing Hilda as he had every night for the past week. He thought back to the night when he first laid eyes on Hilda Sjostedt.

He had parked his old bike in the place near his building where all the other tenants' bikes were parked. The landlord had told him if he parked it anywhere else on the property he would find it in the trash the next day, broken into pieces. Since it was his only mode of transportation, Albin gladly complied with the landlord's rules.

As he walked toward the door of his ground floor flat, he could hear a woman's voice humming a lullaby. He didn't know of any small children living nearby. He went toward the sound and found a young woman, a girl near his age, parking her bike on the other side of the building next door. He listened to the lilting melody for a few minutes longer.

> *Doo doo doo doobakaruula,*
> *Mistas tiesit tanne tuula?*
> *Pitkin tieten myoden tuulin,*
> *Keppi kadessa keikudellan.*

— went the words to the lullaby. (A translation can be found at the end of this chapter.)

Impatient to meet the person with the lovely voice, Albin called out, "Hello, young woman."

The voice out of the near darkness startled her. She stopped humming and jumped slightly. "Who is it? Who's there?"

"It's just me, Albin, your neighbor... I'm sorry... I didn't mean to scare you."

"You didn't scare me", the woman said.

"Do you have a name?" Albin asked.

"Of course, silly, everybody has a name. I am Hilda Sjostedt. I live here with my brother, John Sarvimaara, and he is well known around here," she replied in a defensive tone. She began to walk toward the apartment's main door.

"Wait," Albin called out. "I'm really sorry I startled you then, Hilda Sjostedt. Please forgive me."

"Well, you didn't startle me," Hilda said. She was getting a little edgy over this stranger who really did surprise her, but she'd never admit it.

Albin came a little closer and in the dim light he could see Hilda was a beautiful woman. Her dark auburn curls hung down to her waist from a large slip comb holding a bunch of her hair in place on top of her head. She had skin the color of rich cream and it looked as if it might be just as smooth should he touch it. Her lips were naturally pink and had a curve to them that Albin found irresistible. He could imagine kissing those pouting lips.

Albin's eyes took in the rest of this lovely woman and he could tell she had a good figure beneath a peach colored dress made of some kind of rustling fabric that made a swishing sound when she walked. Her full skirt swept the ground and a fitted bodice accentuated her ample breasts. He wondered how women could ride their bicycles with all that fabric and billowing skirts.

Albin then concentrated on Hilda's face. Even in the dim light he could see she had luxurious black eyebrows and long, curling eyelashes. And then he noticed that Hilda had one brown eye and one blue. Albin cleared his throat when he realized he had been staring. As if she could read his mind Hilda said, "You are wondering why I have one brown eye and one blue, aren't you?"

"Ah, well…" Albin stammered. "I didn't mean to stare."

"It's all right. A lot of people think it's odd, but I can explain it," She got up close to Albin's face so he could see better and said, "I was very little and wondered where the steam in the tea kettle was coming from. I got too close to the spout and burned myself in that eye which is how it turned color. But I can still see out of it."

"Hmm-mm. A Swede, eh?" Albin said, picking up on her slight accent and choosing not to further pursue the strange eye colors.

"So, what's wrong with being a Swede?" Hilda said.

"Oh, nothing…nothing at all," Albin stammered. "I am just surprised to see a Swedish woman this far east — away from the coast. Most Swedes are settled to the west.

Albin needn't have been so surprised. At one time, Finland was under Sweden's rule. In those days many Swedes crossed over into Finland, and vice versa, each believing the other country offered more opportunities for young people. In fact, life was hard living anywhere this far north where so much snow fell in winter and the temperatures nearly always hovered near zero. In the cold, cold winters, most people traveled on cross-country skis or horse-drawn sleighs.

Hilda said, "Well, it's not that far, you know. My brother John and his wife, Mary, were also immigrants a few years ago. They changed their name to Sarvimaara when they came here. I haven't decided if I want to change my name or not but I probably won't. I am proud of being Swedish."

Hilda explained that she was from a large family—she had ten siblings—and her brother offered to take her, the youngest of the children, to live with them. Some of the other siblings were already married and living with their spouses, and the few single children left were scattered among other kind relatives after the death of their parents.

"I'm sure you are right, Hilda," he said. "I'm sure the Swedes are very good people. At least they are not Russian." Then he realized it might not be proper to express a political opinion to someone he had just met. "But since you now live in Finland, you are now a Finn girl."

Hilda began to giggle at his remark. "I guess you're right. So, if that is the case, are you always a Finn boy?"

They both laughed. The ice broken, Albin became a little more comfortable talking to this beautiful Swedish-Finn girl.

They stood there for a few moments longer while Albin shifted his weight from one foot to the other. As if reading his mind again Hilda said, "My legs are tired, too, from all the walking I do at work. There is a bench over by the front porch. Let's go rest and talk a little more."

Hilda could see nothing improper about sitting next to this young man—boy actually—and she beckoned him to follow her. She really wanted to get closer to him to see if those huge bulging muscles in his arms were real. She could imagine those arms folded around her in a tight embrace. She blushed at her own sensual thoughts

"So Mr. Albin, do you have a last name?"

"I am Albin Putkonen," he said, pulling himself up to full height before he sat down. "My birth place is Mikkeli, a couple of days north of here. I have not traveled much, only between there and here, but I once went with my father to Saamiland that had been his home. Some people still call it Lapland."

Hilda cringed when Albin mentioned Lapland. Her brother had nothing nice to say about Saamiland, the mostly frozen area close to the North Pole. John seemed to hold much disdain for its inhabitants.

What John actually said was: "When the Lapps

began to travel south out of their birth land, they infiltrated and intermarried with the Finns and as a result, with all the intermingling of the races, we now have a bunch of idiots in our midst."

"Oh, John, you are such an ignorant man," his wife upbraided him.

"No, Mary, it is true. They are muddying our pure lineage. Those Laplanders are directly descended from the caveman. Who knows what kind of inferior blood courses through their veins. We already know some of them are direct descendants of the Mongolians. Just flower-picking trash," he spat as he stomped out of the room.

Hilda remembered her brother's stern language. She had wondered at the time: "Cavemen? Mongolians? Are those people really bad? Aren't we all descended from cave men?"

Aloud, she said to Albin, "Isn't Lap—, I mean, Saamiland, the home of the big reindeer?"

"Oh, yes, Hilda. You have never seen a more beautiful animal, but they're not too bright. In fact they're pretty stupid, really," Albin continued.

Hilda wondered, "Maybe John has the Laplanders confused with their native reindeer." She grinned broadly.

"Did I say something funny?"

"No," she said and quickly wiped the smile from her face. "What kind of work do they do up there?"

"Well, I don't know, but my father said most of the men were farmers. It's a hard way to make a living. Some of them herd reindeer but that's also a very hard life."

Albin changed the subject. "I am a carpenter and learned to work with wood at Arvo Makela's shop just this year. Making beautiful cabinets and finishing the inside of homes with fine wood is a good way to make a living."

There was a glow about Albin as he talked about his work. He was obviously proud of what he did and Hilda hoped she could see Albin's cabinets one day. She thought about how wonderful it would be to have a beautiful home on a hill filled with fine furniture and exquisite wood cabinets to display fine porcelain and china. She figured she would have to marry a very rich man to have all the things she wanted. This Albin was probably not going to be very rich in his lifetime. Unless he became an entrepreneur like her brother, she mused.

Albin had recognized the name of Hilda's brother as soon as she said it. He now knew Hilda lived with one of the richest men in the city, but she was still working outside of her home in addition to helping out with the housework and cooking. Albin wondered why her brother made her work so hard when he had so much money.

John Sarvimaara was known as a strict man who employed many of the townspeople at his factory. He was generous with his employees and paid them well as long as they could keep up with his personal rules—rules that were extremely harsh by anyone's standards. The men had to cut their hair in a certain way and were not allowed to drink liquor or smoke tobacco, even when they were away from the factory and on their own time. Women employees were not allowed to talk to the men at the factory except to convey information about their work. There would be no fraternizing between men and women at work or even after work with Sarvimaara as the head of the company.

Cussing was not permitted and employees were encouraged to tell on their friends if they heard them cuss outside of work or engage in any of Sarvimaara's "sins". In truth, most of the people in town lived in fear of John Sarvimaara. Some said he was a bully, others said he was simply a good businessman who demanded the best of his employees.

Sarvimaara also owned much property around the city, including Albin's apartment house located in back of the building where Hilda lived. The flat, that he and a few friends of his from school had just moved into a couple of months before, was very small with only three small rooms. It was crowded and Hilda's brother charged a hefty rent for the cramped quarters. But it would have to do until Albin could save enough for something better.

The same strict rules that existed in the factory applied to Sarvimaara's many rentals as well. Tenants were held to a higher standard when they rented from Sarvimaara. When it came down to it, John Sarvimaara was not one of Helsinki's beloved citizens, but he supported so many families they tolerated his eccentricities.

Hilda felt like her work was on a par with Albin's job. They both worked with their hands, toiling at the whim of others, working for a small paycheck each week. When Albin asked what kind of work she did Hilda told him she made garments in a small factory.

"I sew pieces of fabric together on a sewing machine," Hilda said. "Not really so grand as creating things out of beautiful wood, but it is interesting to me. It's creative even though we have patterns to follow," Hilda said.

"When all the pieces have been sewn together, they finally become a blouse or dress. The last seamstress to sew her piece gets to see the completed project. I just started working there so what I do isn't very exciting."

Hilda didn't tell Albin she hoped one day to become the Floor Boss, a goal that would put her into a higher salary and a position in which workers would look up to her. Floor Boss had many rewards attached to the title in addition to a higher salary, but her goals didn't stop there. Someday she wanted to own the garment factory and be someone important like her brother, John.

She didn't think it proper to talk about her ambitions to this boy she had only just met so she left him thinking she was happy with her little sewing job.

Just then they heard her brother John shouting out of one of the apartment's upstairs windows-- it was more like a bellow: "Hilda? Is that you out there? You had better get in here now. No decent lady is out at night in this city."

Hilda said to Albin. "That's my brother. I'd better get up there now or it will be a switch to my hinder," and with that, she disappeared through the doorway. Albin decided then and there that his new friend was living with a very bad man. But, since the man was also his landlord, Albin would keep his opinions to himself... for now.

Finnish Lullaby Translation

(The first line has little meaning, but is more like a mother simply humming.)

Second line: *How did you know to get here?*

Third line: *Along the road I traveled*

Fourth line: *Swinging my cane in my hand.*

ALBIN'S LETTERS

Chapter 2

Hilda went straight to her bedroom after greeting Mary and John. She didn't want to talk to them because she might give away the fact that she had been talking to a boy outside when John yelled at her from the window. Worse yet, she had been talking to someone who was probably the only man in town who didn't work at her brother's factory.

She didn't know how she would keep it from her brother. She was sure there were neighbors walking by tonight who had seen the two of them sitting together on the bench. Somebody was sure to tell John about them. Gossip was this town's favorite pastime.

Hilda went straight to her desk and unlocked the drawer where she kept her journal. She kept the key on a chain around her neck for fear John would one day go into her room and find her secret writings. Hilda thought for a minute about Albin, the boy she had just met. This Albin was handsome, very muscular and had the most beautiful blue eyes she had ever seen, topped by thick, brown eyebrows. His hair was blond and wavy, with one small lock that fell over his forehead. A better looking man she had never seen. Albin was truly the kind of man that Hilda dreamed about as she was growing up.

Besides being handsome and strong, Albin was intelligent as well as industrious. The way he talked about his trade and the way he described his woodworking with such passion was proof enough to her that not all young men who didn't work at her brother's factory were lazy bums.

For many nights Hilda could think of nothing but Albin. She wondered, "Is this what falling in love is all about?" Could a chance meeting with a boy she had never seen before stir these feelings in her in such a short amount of time?

Hilda didn't go down for supper. When Mary knocked on her door and asked if she was all right, Hilda said, "I'm okay, Mary. I am just so weary after working so hard today. I really think I should just go to bed. I will get up early and eat a big breakfast, I promise."

Mary wasn't sure her usually ravenous sister-in-law was feeling well. It wasn't like her not to be the first one at the table and eat every morsel on her plate. But she didn't argue. She just said, "Okay, Hilda. But if you are not feeling well, I should be told." Not hearing another sound from the room she left to join her husband.

"I don't know, John. Maybe Hilda is just having growing pains. It's not like her to skip a meal. Any meal. I'll check on her later."

"Better she skip a lot of meals. She doesn't do enough around here to earn what she does eat", John said. "Mary, you spoil the girl. My sister was supposed to work for her room and board when she came here. I don't see her do much of anything these days except go to her little sewing job and visit with her friends in the park.

"Who was that she was talking to this evening down on the bench? Could it have been a boy? She will become a prostitute if she's allowed to linger outside at night when she should be in here helping you with the housework."

"Oh, John, you are so suspicious. Hilda is a nice girl. You'll see. Someday she will make us proud."

Hilda lay on her bed in the near darkness. She had drawn the shade to block out the remaining twilight. She could feel her breasts through the thin cotton nightgown. Her nipples swelled and became hard. She wondered if men had similar feelings.

She fell asleep thinking of Albin and reindeer in a field of wildflowers. She dreamed Albin was on top of her, kissing her neck, kissing her breasts…he had slipped her nightgown over her head. His muscular body melted into hers and she dreamed of being lifted upward, his hands were all over her taking care of Hilda's passion. She awakened with a scream, startling Mary who came running to her room.

"Are you all right, Hilda? Did you have a bad dream?" She asked.

The dream fresh in her mind, Hilda said, "Yes, Mary. I guess I had a nightmare."

She would never tell Mary what a passionate dream she had about a boy she'd only just met. But she desperately wanted to tell somebody.

Albin walked around the landlord's big house and covered the short distance to the apartment where his friends were already sitting down to their evening meal.

"Hey, Albin. How come you are so late? Were you out with your girlfriend?" Eero Tynjala, the oldest of the five boys teased.

They all laughed and Arturi, the youngest roommate, said, "Nah — Albin is too shy to have a girlfriend. He wouldn't know what to do with her!"

Big laugh again, after which Albin spoke up, "Well, if you morons have to know, I was outside talking to a girl. We just met and you will all be jealous when you meet her — IF I let you meet her!"

More laughter and then Uho Lipponen wiped the sauce from his mouth and cleared his throat. "Albin, it may have been awhile since your father explained the facts of life to you. I think you and I should have a little talk before you meet this girl again."

Albin said, "Hey, Uho. What makes you think you know more than I do about those things? I don't see any girls hanging around you. You have more boys running after you than girls!"

With that remark, Uho was on his feet, fists clenched. "You take that back, Albin!"

The others had to pull Uho off of Albin before blood flowed.

"Okay," said Albin. "I didn't mean to say that. But I don't need your help about matters of love. I'm sure I'll know what to do when the time comes."

Peace finally settled in the little flat, and Don

Kahilainen, the quiet roommate, said, "Let's lower our voices. The other tenants can hear us when we speak loudly. These walls are very thin, yanno."

But Arturi wanted to hear more from Albin about the girl he had just met.

"Please, Albin, tell me what she looks like. How old is she?"

Albin finished his supper and after clearing the dishes from the table (it was his turn this night) he went to the shabby sofa and sat down next to Arturi.

He spoke just to him. The others were holding books and magazines, pretending to read, but all the while they were listening intently to Albin's words.

Albin lowered his voice and said: "You wouldn't believe how beautiful she is." And then on impulse he said: "She is a Swede." He went on to describe Hilda's beautiful hair, her smooth creamy complexion, her curvy figure and full breasts, and her blue-brown eyes.

"Well that's nice about the full breasts and nice hair and skin and all, but what do you mean, blue-brown eyes?" Art asked.

"Well, one is blue and one is brown," said Albin.

The four boys sitting on chairs around the room all dropped what they were reading.

"Okay," Uho said, "That's not possible, Albin. You either have two brown eyes or you have two blue eyes."

"No, no—it's true. Really. She told me when she was very little she tried to look into the spout of a teakettle and she burned her right eye. She can still see out of it, but it is brown."

"I gotta see that," said Eero. The others grunted, and all agreed this new friend of Albin's must be a curiosity.

Albin's Letters

Chapter 3

Hilda and Albin met again the next night. Then they met again a third and a fourth time. By then Albin knew he was in love with Hilda and he knew she had feelings for him.

On that fourth night Albin and Hilda were sitting on the bench, talking and kissing—mostly kissing—when Albin heard the upstairs window creak ever so slightly. He jumped up and ran around to the other side of the building, just as John plunged from the second story window and crashed into a large bush by the front door.

He came up sputtering and swearing and when he could catch his breath he said to Hilda, "I knew you were down here kissing that boy. Where did he go? Did he run away just now?"

"I don't know what you're talking about, John. There was no boy here," Hilda lied.

John wasn't convinced. He knew she was lying. He brushed the leaves and dirt from his clothing, still muttering to himself. "When I catch him, I'll break his neck. Then I'll have him tarred and feathered!"

When Albin saw Hilda the next night, he said, "I'm glad your brother didn't build the house three stories high. He would have broken his neck if he'd fallen from the third floor!"

The young lovers continued to meet after work but now they made an effort to be more discreet — and more quiet. They began meeting around the back-side of the house. They also began to talk more openly about their hopes and dreams for the future. Hilda wanted to have a houseful of children, which may explain why she was humming a lullaby the first night Albin met her.

Albin also wanted a family but his dreams went beyond that. He wanted to own his own business and build big beautiful houses that rich people would buy. He couldn't see that happening as long as he worked for someone else. Other things would have to happen first, like sailing to America. It was something many young people were thinking about in those days.

One evening, Hilda and Albin sat outside in the shadows behind the house. Whispering softly, they shared a now familiar embrace as they kissed and held one another. Suddenly, John came rushing through the back door. He was furious!

"Slut!" John shouted as he grabbed Hilda by the hair. "Get inside, you bad, bad girl!"

Hilda quickly obeyed.

"And, YOU! You heathen!" He yelled as he shook his fist at Albin. "I know who you are! People have been talking. Don't you show your face around here again. I also know where you live and as of now you are evicted. Get your belongings off my property. And furthermore, if you know what's good for you, you will leave Helsinki."

Albin was devastated. He didn't care about the apartment; he could find another flat. But he was afraid John would keep him from ever seeing Hilda again.

When he went to work the next day, he discovered he was also out of a job. Hilda's brother had gone right over to Mr. Makela's house after his confrontation with the young lovers and threatened to put him out of business unless he fired Albin Putkonen.

Albin wondered how Mr. Sarvimaara knew so much about him. He suspected it might have been one of his roommates. They all worked at the factory.

Young men like to brag and gossip like old women. They feel important knowing privileged information. And, the more these stories are passed on, the more exaggerated and juicier they become. Albin was aware of this and figured news about him and Hilda necking in her brother's back yard was now all over town.

Hilda cried all night after John's ugly scene. She was embarrassed about what the talk might be in the neighborhood, but even more, she was hurt and heartbroken that she might never see Albin again.

She went to John and begged, "Please don't drive Albin away, dear brother. It wasn't his fault; I was encouraging him. I'm in love with Albin. I will surely be a spinster if I can't marry Albin," she said tearfully.

But no amount of tears and pleading would budge the stubborn John. He even shut out Mary when she pleaded with him on Hilda's behalf.

"I will not have you questioning my authority or my judgement! I am the head of this house and I am done talking about it!" He slammed the door on the way out. Sounds of women wailing still rang in his ears as he stomped off to the nearest tavern. A couple of tins of beer would calm him down. "Oi, oi, oi! Women! Why do they always have to talk back? Life would be so much easier if they would just keep their mouths shut and obey their men."

Albin knew he'd never find work or a place to live in this town. All of the residents were in some way connected to John's factory and they were afraid to befriend him.

So he picked up what few belongings he owned, including some of his favorite books and all of his woodworking tools, and hitched a ride to Mikkeli. His sister Olga and his brother, August lived there and he was sure they would help him get established. Besides those two siblings, his father, Hermann, and another brother and sister, Adam and Hilma, also still lived in Mikkeli, so if it became too crowded at Olga's he was sure one of the others would take him in. His father remarried after Albin's mother died and they had another son so he knew there would be no room for him at their place. Olga would be his best bet.

She had offered him a place to live after Albin graduated from school, and now he planned to take her up on her offer if it was still good. He said goodbye to his friends at the apartment and promised he would write a letter to them so they would know where he was. They told Albin they were sorry to see him leave. They gave him gifts and said they would miss him.

Their kind gestures encouraged him, but could not mend Albin's broken heart. After he settled in at Olga's he went out looking for work. It took a couple of days but then he found a job making wooden butter churns for dairy farmers in the area. The dairy industry was important to Finland's economy, so anything to do with it meant financial security.

The following Sunday, Albin could stand it no longer. He followed his heart and paid to use his brother's horse and wagon and set out for Helsinki to see Hilda.

He went straight to Hilda's garment factory and waited there until evening. He stopped Hilda as she came through the door and wrapped his arms around her, a bold act in front of her fellow workers, but he felt so strongly about his love for her that he didn't care.

"Oh, Albin," Hilda cried. "I have been so worried about you. I didn't know what happened to you."

Albin spoke softly as he held her, "Shh, my darling. It is all okay now. I live in Mikkeli with my sister. I have other family there, too. I just wanted you to know I am all right. He stepped back and took her hands in his.

"But you, dear Hilda, how are you doing with John? I feel so badly that I have caused you problems with your family."

She squeezed his hands. "Oh, Albin, please don't worry about me. I will be all right."

"I've made a decision," Albin said. "I decided that with all the unrest in our country, we'll never be happy until we leave here and go to America or Canada. I have read and heard about the Finns who left here and settled in Canada. Or we could just settle somewhere in the United States. I am willing to leave my homeland to find a place where we can live without fear."

And so it was settled. Albin would leave for America just as soon as he earned enough money to pay his passage. Hilda would wait until she heard from Albin and then she would board a ship for America and meet him there.

ALBIN'S LETTERS

Chapter 4

When Albin settled into his little room at his sister's house in Mikkeli it was the first time he had space all to himself; he didn't have to share it with siblings or friends.

There were other advantages to living in Mikkeli. For one thing there was the sauna, which was an extremely popular activity throughout Finland. Only now in Mikkeli, he found more time to use one.

One room in every house, or in a small building outside the main house, was dedicated to this unique steam bath called a sauna. A wood fired stove with the fire box below and a crib to hold rocks on top was set in a corner of a small room. Benches or risers were built along one wall. As water was poured over the hot rocks a burst of steam would rise and the temperature would get unbearably hot, nearly 175 to 200 degrees Fahrenheit. The bathers would take up birch tree switches that had been cut from trees earlier in the day and allowed to dry out. They beat themselves and each other with the switches to make the blood rise to the surface of their skin. As the bathers stepped higher onto the risers, they gradually made it to the top shelf and stayed there as long as they could stand it and then they would run from the building and jump into the snow, or into a nearby cold lake or pond.

There was a difference of opinion on how sauna bathing should take place. One was that the men would go into the sauna first while the women stayed in the kitchen and made coffee and sweet breads. Then after the men dressed and returned to the main house the women would take their turn. Some groups would play cards or other games after the sauna.

The young people's version of this was that everybody would go into the sauna together, naked, and frolic in the snow, then retreat to rooms or cabins where frolicking of another sort ensued. In both versions the participants would later dance to music played by someone with a harmonica or on a piano if there were one available. One of the couples had purchased a new invention by Thomas Edison called a phonograph on which music could be played from a cylinder. On special occasions there would be live accordion music for their dancing and a little vodka or beer would be served for refreshment.

Albin learned how to dance the polka and the schottische as soon as he could walk and now next to woodworking and sauna baths, dancing was his favorite pastime. He only wished that Hilda could be in his arms to learn his favorite dances. He missed her so much.

Albin wrote to Hilda every day. He didn't know if her brother would intercept his letters so he sent them to Hilda's friend, Freda. Freda knew what a strict guardian Hilda's brother was and promised to keep Hilda's secret. They would meet after work and when Hilda had finished reading Albin's letters Freda would take them back to her house and keep them for Hilda.

Hilda spent many hours thinking about Albin and decided she would put up with her brother's mean temper no longer. She wrote to Albin and said, "Make room for me in that little room of yours. I'm catching a ride to Mikkeli tomorrow. We will be together, Albin, no matter how hard it will be. I have some money saved that John knows nothing about. It will sustain us until I can find a job."

Albin's sister Olga was eager to have Hilda stay at her house. Another woman to talk to would be nice, and Hilda could help with the household chores to help pay for her room and board.

And so the couple settled in, without benefit of matrimony. They spent many hours sharing thoughts about what they would do when they someday moved to America.

On sauna nights, they joined in with the others and pretended they were just one of the old married couples. However, this wasn't exactly the way Hilda saw herself as she grew into womanhood. She thought about what John said that night he stormed out of the house. Maybe he was right. Maybe she really was a bad, bad girl. Hilda didn't say anything to Albin about what she was thinking but she hoped one day he would ask her to marry him. Albin was thinking he should ask Hilda to marry him when the trouble started all across Finland.

Chapter 5

In 1809 Finland became part of the Russian
Empire. Most of the Finns hated being under
Russian rule but they had little in the way of ideas
for a change. In 1899 Russia launched a program of
"Russification" in Finland, designed to force Finns to
adopt the Russian language and culture.

Many of the Finns were vehemently opposed
to this Russian-driven movement. For one thing, a
lot of unrest was caused by the changes in religious
teachings. Extremely conservative members of a
religious movement, established in the early 1800s,
clashed with Finns at the other end of the spectrum:
Finns who denounced their belief in God and
adopted the Communist philosophy.

And then the most controversial edict came
down, especially for young men across Finland,
Estonia and other nearby countries under Russian
rule: Men were required to serve in the Russian
army. Many of them decided to flee the country
where they had lived all their lives to avoid military
service.

Just after the turn of the century, a group
of Finns arrived in British Columbia, Canada,

searching for a place where they could live in peace without the government or the church interfering. The immigrants sought to establish their own Utopia on Malcolm Island, located at the southeastern end of Johnstone Strait near the north end of Vancouver Island on the far western shore of Canada.

A Finnish philosopher and newspaper man named Matti Kurrika joined the immigrants to help organize the effort. The group of Finns and Kurikka founded the Kalevan Kansa Colonization Company. A newspaper named Aika was established in the Vancouver Island city of Nanaimo, British Columbia. Aika, which translates to "Times", was later moved to a new settlement.

The group of colonists and Kurrika arranged a meeting with the British Columbia government to formally acquire Malcolm Island. A celebration called the Juhannus was held by the new settlers in June 1902 to celebrate the new colony, and the group named the colony "Sointula", which translates to Place of Harmony.

In some of his articles Kurrika wrote about Finnish women who had been held like slaves by their husbands for generations and treated as possessions. He blamed the church for encouraging this behavior of men toward women.

After reading about Sointula, Albin wasn't
sure this is where he would settle with Hilda once
he sent for her, but something about the stories he
heard and read intrigued him to the point of at least
investigating the possibility. When he thought about
Hilda, which was every day of his waking life as well
as in his dreams, he knew her to be a free spirit, a
woman who met life head on without fear. Albin
realized Kurrika might have been talking about his
beloved Hilda who had been held back, discouraged
from following her dreams, by her domineering
brother.

Albin wasn't the only Finn who was dissatisfied
with life in his country. Most of them had what
they felt were good reasons to leave. Boarding ships
headed for America became a way out. The Finnish
exodus had already begun.

ALBIN'S LETTERS

Chapter 6

Albin decided to get on the next ship to America, but felt that Hilda would not be safe in Mikkeli with him gone. He convinced her to return to her brother's house in Helsinki and stay there until he could send for her. They planned to meet in Chicago.

"It will only be a couple of months at the most," Albin told Hilda. "I will write every day to let you know where I am and what I am doing."

The couple packed their belongings and said their good-byes to Olga. She tearfully hugged the couple and said, "I shall miss you, but someday I will be in America, too. We will look forward to many sauna parties in the new world."

It was hard for Albin to leave his family again. His brother August wanted to leave on the same ship but had pressing business in Mikkeli and so would not be leaving for at least one more year.

Albin and Hilda waved goodbye to friends and family, hoping they would meet again someday. They rode with a farmer into Helsinki.

Albin went to stay with his old friends and

Hilda went straight to her brother's house. It was not a joyful reunion as far as John was concerned. But Hilda was very happy to see Mary. They hugged and kissed and Hilda cried when Mary said, "You are like my daughter. I thought I had lost you forever!"

"Oh, Mary, I have missed you as well." Then she whispered, "But I will leave for America as soon as Albin sends for me so it will only be for a short while."

She hoped John hadn't heard her mention Albin's name. It would turn into a fight if he had. Tired as she was from her trip, she didn't want to start an argument.

She told Mary that Albin would be writing every day to tell her where he was and what kind of work he found there.

"But Hilda, what if he doesn't find a good job? What if he has to come back?"

"Don't worry, Mary. I am sure my Albin will be ready to send for me in a few months. Meanwhile I will keep busy here and try to keep out of John's way.

"I must go now and say goodbye to Albin. He is leaving on a boat to Scotland to get on the big ship to America." And with that, she was out the door and running for Albin's house, a large duffle bag slung over her shoulders.

She caught him as he was leaving.

"Did you remember to take all your shaving things?, Hilda asked him. They may not have the kind of soap you like in America."

"I think they have everything I will like and more, Hilda. After all, it has been called a bright new world with gold in the streets."

Hilda said, "Well, just in case…" and handed Albin the bag she was carrying. It was filled with money, mostly in gold coins. Albin was aghast. "Where did you get all this money, Hilda? Did you steal it from your brother?"

Hilda laughed: "Oh, no, Albin. It is my money that I've been saving for a long time. I made a few investments — loaned money to friends who paid me back over the years with interest. I kept careful track and there is nothing illegal about it. This is only part of what I have in my account at the bank."

Albin couldn't believe his eyes and ears. "But Hilda, there must be a thousand dollars in here," he said as he lifted the heavy leather bag.

"More or less…" Hilda replied.

Albin now had more respect than ever for his beautiful and intelligent Hilda.

Now Albin had more than enough money for passage to America and some left over to get settled in the new country.

Hilda's sister-in-law managed to smooth over the ruffled feelings of her husband at the prospect of having Hilda back living with them again. John still wasn't sure he wanted Hilda to stay. "What if she's pregnant? Then we'll have her and her boyfriend's bastard to support."

John needn't have worried. Hilda had been very careful not to get pregnant. She didn't want to bring a child into the world born out of wedlock. Even though she was in love with Albin, life would be tough enough without having an extra mouth to feed.

Chapter 7

Hilda waved goodbye to her sweetheart at the dock where he boarded a small boat headed for Scotland along with a few friends he met in Mikkeli. At the last minute, two of his roommates, Eero and Arturi Tynjala, decided to join Albin. The young men joined a few other draft evaders in their late teens, and sailed at the end of May on the SS Laurentian from Glasgow, Scotland. They arrived at Ellis Island in New York Harbor on June 5, 1902.

The journey across the Atlantic made Albin and his buddies seasick almost non-stop during the five day trip. The ships' galley served wonderful meals but none of them felt much like eating. They ate only enough to sustain them and then walked rigorously on the decks to keep up their strength.

Albin wrote, "Dearest Hilda, We have arrived in America and we were almost sent back home because they said they didn't want any more single men. Then, a miracle happened."

When they went to check through customs on Ellis Island, Albin and the others, last to leave the ship, were told they could not stay. The quota for unmarried men had been filled and they would have to leave on the same ship that was returning to Scotland within the hour.

Albin and his friends awaited their fate. All kinds of crazy thoughts went through his head. He thought about jumping into New York Harbor and swimming to shore. He was a strong swimmer and would have no problem getting to the beach. Then he looked over at the customs officers, all of whom were wearing side arms, and thought he might not make it over the railing without getting shot.

Just then a huge man with bulging muscles and wearing a Russian fur hat came up to the customs table where the officers had stopped the men. The big man said, "I have room for a couple more men to fill my quota. Any of you guys know how to log a forest?" He boomed.

They all shouted, "Yes!" even though most of them had never been near a logging operation and had manicured hands as groomed and delicate as a woman's, except for Albin. His hands were strong and calloused from years of working with copper and lumber and before that a young lad working alongside his father on the farm.

He motioned them toward the small skiff

alongside the dock and said, "Get in. We're wasting daylight here. You can bring your documents and I'll get you through Canadian customs at the border. I'll vouch for you."

American customs officers knew the big Swede to be a man of his word. Ole Johanson had recruited young men right off the boat who didn't have jobs elsewhere. It didn't matter that they had never worked in the woods before. He would teach them everything they needed to know. The officers urged the group to go with him if they wanted.

The young men gathered their papers and clambered into the small boat and hung on as the skipper and his crew of rowers pulled away from the dock. None of them had time to understand what logging a forest might mean, but they knew they didn't want to return to Finland, so figured they'd soon find out.

When they reached shore, Johanson handed each of them a Ushanka, a warm hat made of fur, so they could keep their heads warm. Johanson believed if your head was warm and your feet were dry you would remain in good health. And you could fell more trees!

The rag-tag outfit was herded into a large horse-drawn wagon as it left the waterfront heading north towards Canada, Albin turned around just in time to see the Statue of Liberty fade into the distance.

At the border, the Canadian officials thought Albin, at four foot eleven inches tall, was a child—until he turned around and they could see the mustache and two-day beard growth on his face. He was short, but muscular and strong. Still, the boss didn't believe he was strong enough to handle the large cross-cut saws.

He asked Albin: "Can you cook?"

Knowing his cooking skills were limited but afraid he'd be turned away if he said that, he replied, "Of course!"

And so it was settled. Albin would earn his paycheck on the chow wagon. It didn't make him feel less of a man and it was a job. He also had a secret he didn't share right away with the boss. Albin was well known as an accomplished wrestler when he was in school. He would soon become legendary in the logging camps as a free style wrestler.

Some of his Finn buddies knew about Albin's wrestling ability and began to challenge him each evening after supper, taking him aside and asking him not to hurt them, "Just pretend," they pleaded. The other loggers took one look at the diminutive lad from Finland and said, "He doesn't look so tough. Bet I can beat him." Wagers were made among the men on who would win, and then when they saw what Albin could do, how long it would take for him to beat his opponents.

The ante pot grew greater and word spread among other logging camps in the area. Soon Albin had to defend his title among some of the biggest brutes in southern Canada.

But as hard as that was, Albin still found time to write letters to Hilda every night. He told her of his work and of the wrestling matches and he tried to draw a word picture of the beauty he saw in the huge forests.

"Hilda, my love," he began each letter, "You would not believe your eyes at the beauty I wake up to every morning. Next to you, it's the most beautiful sight in the world. My head is filled with the stunning sunrises pouring through the tall evergreens. I have learned the names of all the trees since we began logging across Canada. The one called Douglas Fir is the most valuable and brings the best prices. And the cedar trees, very graceful looking with boughs draping down toward the ground beneath the forest.

"Wild animals are everywhere. So many deer and rabbits and funny looking raccoons that come right up to the cook shack and beg for food, just like little children.

"The mother deer will escort her youngsters to the campsite but stay at the edge of the woods. When one of the little fawns tries to dart out closer to where the loggers are, the mother will run around it and herd it back where it will be safe.

"We don't see too many birds, but we can hear them chattering up high in the canopy. They stay near the tops of the trees but have to watch for predators, like the huge eagles that raid their nests for eggs. When an eagle gets too close, you can hear them making so much noise up there. They may be underdogs but they manage to survive."

"I haven't seen but a couple of bears, but on the first night out the foreman of the crew was mauled by a huge black. He died before we could reach him."

Albin didn't want to worry Hilda so he didn't say any more about wild animals in his midst. He told her about how many of the plants, like the one called "salal", was used in native people's diets. There were berries and ferns that Albin learned to incorporate into foods he served to the loggers. Cranberries, found in the wetlands of the forest floor were much like the lingonberries back home. He found blackberries and very large huckleberries for puddings and other desserts that brought a lot of praise from the loggers.

Night after night he would write to Hilda, hoping that they would soon be together. He never guessed that Hilda would not see his letters for a very long time.

Back in Finland, Hilda was busy with her job at the factory and then after work going to her lonely room and writing many pages in her journal that she would send to Albin as soon as she had an address. She wrote of how sad she was that Albin was not writing to her. She wrote every day of how much she loved and missed him.

"Albin, I will smack you when I see you, for not writing to me all these months. I know you must be having a good time in America or else you would at least tell me where you are and what you have been doing."

"Why did you stop writing? Do you have a job? Are you spending all your spare time in the nightclubs in those decadent cities? Are you fighting off all those women who want to bed you down? Or are you busy bedding down all the women standing around in the streets."

Hilda waited for Albin and remained faithful. One day as Hilda was sitting on the bench outside John's house, her sister-in-law came out and found her crying. "What's taking him so long to send a letter?" She asked Mary.

"Oh, Hilda, America is far away. All of the letters have to come by boat and boats don't have wings, you know." She didn't want to let on that she suspected Hilda's letters might be disappearing as soon as they came through the door and into her husband's hands.

Weeks turned into months and six months had gone by when Hilda decided that Albin must have been killed by American gangsters. She decided the world would soon end — it had become so wild since the turn of the century.

"Oh, Hilda, you must not carry on like this about Albin," Mary said. "You must get on with your life and find another man to keep you happy."

"No!" Hilda sobbed defiantly. "There will never be another man in my life. I'll die an old maid first. Albin is my heaven and earth, the only one who loves me. I know something terrible must have happened to him or I would be getting letters every day. I believe that if he is dead, he died thinking of me. I was the light of his life as he was of mine."

Hilda continued to cry and Mary left her there, thinking maybe Albin was dead. She went to John and said, "That girl will die of a broken heart soon if she doesn't hear from Albin."

John turned his back on Mary and said, "Good riddance."

"John? What are you saying? What is 'good riddance'? Do you know something about Albin?"

John didn't answer right away. He went to the sideboard and got a bottle of brandy and poured himself a full glass. He turned to Mary and said, "Yes, Mary, I know everything. I have been picking up stacks of Albin's letters from the post office. I haven't given them to Hilda because she mustn't be encouraged to think that he will ever be able to send for her.

"Albin Putkonen is a bum. These letters have been coming from many places all over Canada. He isn't even in the United States. He is just wandering from town to town and God knows what he is doing. The letters are dirty by the time they get here.

"I don't believe he loves her. He just has to make her think he does. Hilda would be miserable traveling all around the countryside like that, living from hand to mouth under God-knows-what filthy conditions.

"I am keeping the letters. Maybe some day after she is married to someone else I will give the letters to her. Then she can have a good laugh."

John made Mary promise not to tell Hilda what he said. Mary thought it was criminal but couldn't disobey her husband. She went to her bedroom and cried her heart out for Hilda. Her tears were just as inexhaustible as Hilda's and she spent the better part of that night and most of the next day in her room.

Hilda heard her sister-in-law crying and knocked on her door. "Mary, are you ill? Is there something I can do for you?"

Mary stopped blubbering long enough to say, "I'm fine, Hilda. You will have to do the cooking for the next few days to feed yourself and your brother. I'll be all right. I just need to be alone for awhile."

Hilda wondered if Mary and John were having marital problems and that she might be the cause of it. She didn't know how close that was to the truth.

ALBIN'S LETTERS

Chapter 8

Albin's logging company finally reached the
west coast of Canada where they boarded a large
ship and went to Vancouver Island. From there they
could see the Pacific Ocean and stands of timber
even more verdant than those on the mainland.

Albin knew it must be the marine air that
encouraged the trees to grow so tall and the forest to
grow so thick. His boss was delighted at the sight as
well. He was sure his wealth would continue to grow
if his crew could hold up under the difficult working
conditions. Almost all of the loggers were coming
down with terrible colds and sinus infections due
to the increased humidity. After a few weeks, Albin
and his friends decided to leave the logging outfit
and made their way to Sointula where they knew
the new Utopia was being settled by their Finnish
brothers.

When Albin and the others got to Sointula they
were greeted by the camp's leader, Matti Kurrika,
and another Finn, Art Mikkola, whom Kurrika
had asked to come over to help establish the new
settlement.

Albin introduced himself and his friends as they stepped out of the rowboat — Esko Kekkonen, Gustav Klukainen, and the brothers, Eero and Arturi Tynjala — all of whom accompanied Albin on the ship to New York and worked with the loggers across Canada.

"So happy you could join us," the leader Kurrika said to the new arrivals.

Albin, who was selected by the others to be spokesman, said, "We are pleased to be here and want to know how we can help." Kurrika turned the small group over to one of the other settlers for orientation.

Lempe Kahtilainen, introduced herself to the group. She was tall with green eyes, her long blonde hair in two braids… and appeared to be about 24 years old. She said to Albin, "Follow me. I'll show you where you'll be living until you build your own cabin."

The men looked at each other. One of them silently mouthed, "Build a cabin?"

Albin told the young woman, "I will only stay a short while. I have not discussed a permanent location with my fiancée. She is still in Finland."

Lempe said, "That is fine. You will still have to establish a place for yourself while you are here. It is one of our rules."

Albin thought to himself, "Rules, eh? We left Finland because there were too many rules."

The group entered the small cabin on the edge of the woods. There were a couple of low cots on the dirt floor, no windows, a bucket in the corner which she explained they would want to use in the middle of the night because there were bears that wandered through the camp looking for scraps of food.

"Getting eaten by a bear would not help our cause," Lempe said dryly. "And, of course, you should keep that covered up at all times except when you are using the outhouse," she said, glancing at the flap in front of his pants.

She handed the men a stack of blankets and said, "You will have to sleep two to a bunk to keep warm because it's freezing at night." The men looked at one another and then back at the woman with a poker face.

Esko said, "But none of these men are even attractive to me."

The others laughed. Eero said, "We will grow on

you, Esko."

"When is mealtime?" asked Gustav, the Finn who always thought of his stomach first. It had been awhile since the young men had eaten a decent meal.

Lempe replied, "In about an hour. You will have time to clean up at the wash house you passed on the way here. It's right next to the meeting house."

The group followed Lempe out of the cabin and headed for the lodge. Albin remembered the eight by five foot shack and wondered if it were big enough to hold a sauna.

As if someone inside had heard his thoughts, a young nude couple with bright pink skin, burst through the door and ran to the beach where they plunged into the icy water.

He was about to say something to the others, but as he turned around, the four of them had already shucked their clothes and entered the sauna.

"Hey! Wait for me!" Albin yelled.

Thus their first day at Sointula brought forth a little taste of the old country beginning with a sauna bath, and ending with Loksalota, a sumptuous meal of potatoes, onions and salted salmon in a creamy white sauce with lots of butter. Gustav was about to help himself to more of the wonderful dish, when Albin gave him a look. Gustav looked around and saw that nobody was taking seconds.

Lempe spoke up. "There are some men still out repairing the fishing boats. We will save the leftovers from our meal for them and warm it for them when they come in."

Gustav got up with the others and took his plate to the huge sink where some of the dishwashers were already at work scraping and rinsing. He told Albin, "That Lempe is a fine looking woman, but she sure is tough. I don't want to make her mad. I have to think of a way to get on her good side," and he winked at Albin.

Albin said, "Yeah, Gus. But do you want to get on her good side for a bigger ration of food or is it something else you're after?"

The others laughed at Albin's remark. Esko puckered up his lips and made a kissing sound. "Watch out what you wish for, Gus. You might get it!"

Later that evening the men sat back against a huge log on the beach and thought about their introduction to Malcolm Island.

Albin thought, I don't know what Hilda would think about this new wild land. She might like jumping into the ocean after a sauna. And she would surely enjoy the fine Finnish food these transplanted countrymen could muster up from the meager provisions found in this beautiful wilderness.

"Hilda is a tough woman, too." He thought, "She would be a leader in this new colony. She would have them organized and divided into committees, ready to create a paradise for its inhabitants."

Albin was so proud of Hilda's abilities, he wanted to sing her praises to the stars.

"Dear Hilda, I miss you so much. I am so lonely in this foreign land."

He so wished she could be with him now, sharing his experiences in this wild new place.

He wrote all of his thoughts to her that night after his first day in Sointula. His candle had almost burned out by the time he finished. He fell asleep after he signed his name and the candle died. He dreamed of Hilda and in his dream she was running naked on the beach at Sointula. He was trying to catch her but she was too fast for him. It was as if she had wings. She was flying over the water's edge, waves gently lapping on the shore. And then she turned and waved to him and said, "Goodbye, Albin."

Albin woke with a start. He was shaking all over and then he realized he was sweating profusely and his clothes were wringing wet.

Albin was the first person to come down with scarlet fever at Sointula.

Lempe was assigned to the camp's hospital, one small shack at the far end of the settlement. There were no doctors at the camp, just Lempe who had been studying to be a nurse before she left Finland.

The next day, Gustav came down with the fever. Lempe told Kurrika of the crisis now threatening to take them all if it spread throughout the settlement.

She suggested a quarantine and immediate shipment of Albin's remaining three friends back to Vancouver Island.

Albin and Gustav were too sick to be moved, so they were confined to the hospital for the remainder of their illness.

Lempe stayed with the two men, placing cool wet towels on their heads and all over their bodies as their fevers rose. Ice was brought over from Vancouver Island and ice water was brought to the door of the shed by the colonists. They also brought soups, hardtack and coffee and other foods so Lempe could nourish the two men back to health. Nobody was willing to go inside and help Lempe. The disease was too contagious.

Lempe burned candles from her private supply and incense she purchased from the Chinese community near Victoria, which she was told had healing qualities. Some of the Indian tribes living in the area provided herbs they used in healing their own illnesses. Whether they would work on this white man's disease, they didn't know, but Lempe was willing to try anything.

There were no more outbreaks of scarlet fever on the island. Kurrika gave credit to Lempe whose quick thinking, he believed, saved the colony.

Slowly the two men, who were apparently infected about the same time, began to improve, thanks to Lempe's diligent nursing. She sterilized everything in the shack, and took the men's clothes out and burned them in a fire pit just outside the building. They would be provided with clean, used clothing when they were well enough to leave.

This day finally came and Lempe brought in clothes after which she went out to leave Albin and Gustav to dress in private, Gustav turned to his friend and said, "Oh, Albin, Lempe took care of us when we were naked."

Albin replied, "It's okay, Gus. I'm engaged to be married, and you don't have anything worth bragging about, so I wouldn't be too concerned."

Gustav left the confines of the makeshift hospital feeling as though the whole colony knew that a woman had been bathing him.

Albin took a couple of days to go into the settlement and talk to the residents. He also was looking for a place he'd might like to work should he decide to stay and become a member of the colony. He was thinking they might need a good cook.

He was curious about the meeting house, which, he was told, was recently completed. The structure was built as an apartment house for couples with no children and unmarried settlers.

The third floor was reserved for a meeting room.

Eventually a house was built just for children so they would have a place to go when their parents were at work. The house for children also became a classroom, with teaching provided by those colonists who had studied to be educators.

The colonists logged the trees on the island and hauled them to Vancouver Island where they never seemed to bring much profit. They also tried fishing and, except for their own meals, they never sold enough to pay for the great effort it took. Saltwater fish wasn't even popular among the Finns who were more accustomed to freshwater fish. They salted down the salmon to preserve it, and even after de-brining it wasn't palatable to many of the colonists who had lived inland from the coast.

Still the Sointulans plugged away at being self-sufficient and for the most part succeeded. The wonderful delicacies they enjoyed in the old country were just a memory as they sat down to very basic sustenance, but no one went hungry at Sointula.

Everything was precious on Malcolm Island: Nothing was wasted. Shortly before Albin and his friends arrived a building was constructed to house the printing equipment for the colony's newspaper, Aika, which in Finnish means "times". The times were indeed changing for the transplanted Finns.

As the community's cultural center, Aika addressed questions from the residents, as well as responding to questions in letters from their countrymen in Finland. Many wanted to know more about the rumored free-spirited women in Sointula. There were almost no single women, so it only gave those who resented Kurrika more to complain about. Among the married couples, there were very few separations and divorces.

The colony women had equal say in governmental matters. Back home in Finland, this rule would have been opposed by many, like Hilda's brother who wanted to keep women "in their place." By the same token, women shared in the colony's hard work, such as cutting wood in the forest or working in the communal laundry.

The colony was well organized and completely self-sufficient. In spite of this, however, Sointula was already on the decline when Albin and the others arrived.

While Albin was walking about and talking to

people in the settlement, Gustav was spending time with Lempe who found this new arrival she had nursed back to health getting to be a real pest.

"Gustav, you should be doing some exercise so you will be strong enough to work when you find a job to do here," Lempe told him.

"But I am exercising," Gustav said. "I am following you around and you always walk so very fast."

"Well, I hope you can keep up with me because I'm going to climb to the top of that hill over there and pick berries," she replied, and off she went.

Gustav began to huff and puff as he followed her up the steep incline. "Hey, Lempe, I am not chasing you. You can slow down just a little."

Lempe responded by going even faster. "You are like a goat," Gustav yelled after her as she rounded a bend in the path.

A moment later Gustav almost knocked Lempe down as she stood in the path facing him.

"Who are you calling a goat?" Lempe asked, a smile, more like a smirk, on her face.

"So maybe not a goat," Gustav said, "Maybe just

a big jackrabbit." They stood there grinning at each other and when she spoke, Lempe had softened her voice and said, "Even jackrabbits have feelings."

She took Gustav's hand and said, "You are not really strong enough to be running around like this just out of your sick bed."

Gustav looked into her eyes and really noticed Lempe for the first time. "You have eyelashes like curled bristles on an old paint brush," he said. Lempe waited until Gustav had stopped gasping and then took his face between her hands and kissed him full on the mouth.

After the second and third kiss Gustav managed to catch his breath. "And you have lips as soft as a baby's hand."

On a bed of dry leaves on a small hill at the edge of the Sointulan colony Gustav and Lempe made love for the first time. Lempe stopped Gustav from removing all his clothes and said, "You should not get a chill after what you've been through, Gustav. We can undress later in my cabin in front of the wood stove."

And so the brief lovemaking ended with the promise of better things to come in Lempe's warm cabin. A courtship took place like the colony had never witnessed so far. The new guy was smitten with one of the strongest women, physically and mentally, in the settlement.

They were married a month later on the eve of Albin's departure from Malcolm Island.

Chapter 9

Albin found his old logging outfit when he got
to the island, but a new camp cook had been hired.
There was no work for him there. Albin decided
to head to Vancouver, B.C., and board a ship for
Portland, Oregon, where he heard some new logging
companies were just starting up.

To his dismay there were no openings for
cooks, only axe men and saw operators. The outfits
were still axe logging and Albin didn't think he
could stand the rigors of working with this kind of
logging team.

Wrestling, what he always thought of as a hobby
and not really a job, became a full time occupation.
Once he found that people would pay cash to see
him wrestle, he went out and purchased a new
wrestling costume and several large floor mats.

He found a hall in downtown Portland where
the rent was cheap and paid a printer to make up
posters advertising his wrestling matches. These
he personally posted all over town, to taverns and

dance halls, wherever people gathered, and soon he was taking on some of the strongest men on the west coast. Most of the wrestlers were professionals and he was proud of the fact that as an amateur he was coming out ahead. Now, however, since he was taking money for the matches, he also was considered a professional.

He was gaining notice from logging companies in the area who had heard of the short Finn who wrestled his way across Canada. Not surprisingly, they all wanted in on the action. The companies would sponsor their own boys against the diminutive but mighty Albin.

One of the logging outfits asked Albin if he would like to spend a couple of months in Seattle. There were a lot of eager young men up there who had just missed out on the Alaska gold rush. It might be profitable for Albin to give it a try.

So Albin, anxious to make money wherever and however he could, went with the man who told him about the city of the seven hills and the many loggers and fishermen who needed entertainment while they were in town. There were many brothels and the Pantages Theater attracted a lot of vaudeville acts from all over the world. What they needed were some sporting events, like boxing and wrestling matches. This was a town just waiting for somebody like Albin Putkonen. The little Finn was in his element.

Albin enjoyed winning many of his matches and was making a lot of money in Seattle, but he missed the small town feel of Portland with its much slower pace. So he went back across the Columbia River and settled once more near downtown and signed up for matches almost every night of the week. It was a rigorous schedule but Albin was up for it.

One day he was offered a contract by the U.S. Wrestling Association to appear in contests across the United States. The agent who contacted Albin and signed him up said he would be a very wealthy man someday. Albin was fooled into believing fame and fortune would smile upon him as he wrestled his way across the country. The agent told Albin that as his manager he would collect a 50% commission of the total purse on the night of the match.

Rocko Pulaski, in fact, collected 80% of every purse. Then he told Albin he would still have to cough up another 10% for his room and board. It took some time for Albin to discover he was being cheated by this man who pretended to be his friend. He wished Hilda, who was always good at deciphering, were here to help him with the figures.

"Dear Hilda, something bad has happened and I wish you could be with me to help me figure out why I am losing money when I am working so hard. Something is wrong…"

When it finally dawned on Albin how he was being taken by the agent, he was furious. An ugly scene took place at an arena in Portland, when Albin confronted Pulaski about why the manager was living well and seemed always to have fancy clothes and big Cuban cigars to smoke with his expensive brandy while Albin was going broke.

He attacked Pulaski and broke his nose in the fight. The manager told him he'd better sleep with one eye open, that he had friends who would "take care" of him.

Almost broke and scared that Pulaski would follow through on his threat, Albin hopped a freight train headed east. He decided to take his chances in Chicago. It was rumored that gangsters ruled the city, but it would be better than staying in town where he knew at least one man wanted him dead.

Albin was not enjoying the train ride across the country. An empty freight car was not as comfortable as a coach with soft seats and blankets. A couple of other men occupied the same car as Albin and he was afraid to go to sleep. They looked like criminals and since Albin didn't carry a gun or any means to protect himself, he did what he thought was best: Stay awake.

However, after several hundred miles, Albin could hold out no longer. His eyes closed. He was dead asleep in minutes.

When he woke up Albin found his money belt had been stolen with the rest of Hilda's money. The thieves had also stolen his pants and shoes. The train was stopped somewhere and since he hadn't yet learned how to read English well, he couldn't make out where he was.

He jumped down from the car and walked over to where a couple of men were standing, smoking cigars. They didn't see Albin coming up to them and were startled to see what they thought was a young boy dressed in a mans' jacket and hat — and no pants or shoes.

It was awkward for Albin. He tried to explain

to them in broken English that he had been robbed. One of the men understood what Albin had just gone through. He had seen it happen with bums riding the rails before. He told Albin, "It's okay, buddy. I'll find a pair of pants for you and some shoes."

Albin understood the sign language and thanked the man, greatly relieved that these were kindhearted men and not more crooks.

He asked the men, "Where are we?"

One of them said, "Kansas, Mister. You're in Topeka, Kansas."

Albin said, "Not Chicago?"

"Oh, no," he laughed, "Chicago's about 600 miles in that direction," and he pointed east down the track.

So now Albin was without money but at least had pants and shoes. He was about 600 miles short of where he wanted to be. He sat down on a box near the track and put his head in his hands.

He didn't feel like his English was good enough to say what he needed to say, so he stood up and pulled his pockets inside out. Then he pointed to his stomach and the men understood what it was Albin was telling them. Empty pockets, empty stomach.

They got on either side of Albin and said, "Come with us." Albin understood that much.

They walked the short distance to the railroad shack and led Albin inside. There on a big stove was a kettle of fragrant, steaming hot beef stew that made Albin's mouth water. The spicy aroma from a pot of coffee made the room smell like home. The men took down a few cups and bowls and a big loaf of bread from a cabinet and served Albin the best meal he had eaten in a very long time. Then one of the men disappeared for a short time and came back with a tall, stocky man who came through the door and, in perfect Finnish, said, "Hello, brother. I am Eero Waali."

Albin was so flabbergasted he couldn't speak. How did the men know he was Finnish? He and Eero began to speak in their native tongue, and for the first time since Sointula, Albin felt as if he was truly among friends.

The rest of the evening was spent with Albin telling his new friend all that had happened to him since he got off the boat. Albin bared his soul.

He told about his experiences with the logging camps, the wrestling matches, the adventures at Sointula and finally the bad situation with the wrestling agent in Portland that drove him to head for Chicago. He told Eero about Hilda waiting back in Finland for him to send for her.

Eero Waali listened politely, and when Albin had run out of breath, he said, "Albin, you have been through a terrible time since you left Finland, but you should know that there are a lot of good things about this country. You may have had some bad experiences, but you will find out America is really a good place to be. You will have more friends here than enemies."

Albin was grateful for Eero's thoughtful assessment of what he had been through. For the first time since he decided to leave Finland, Albin felt like he had made the right choice.

Eero took Albin to his house for the night. He said there wouldn't be another freight train coming through until morning so he may as well get a good night's sleep. Albin expressed concern about making it back to the tracks to get on another train, and Eero told him not to worry, he would see that he would be there on time.

Early the next morning, Albin was climbing onto an eastbound freight car. He bade a warm goodbye to a fellow Finn named Eero and thanked him for giving him hope. He promised he would send him a letter when he got to Chicago.

He would remember to tell Hilda about losing his pants and then getting an unexpected warm welcome in a little town in Kansas. He would write her a letter as soon as he got to Chicago.

Albin's Letters

Chapter 10

Hilda finally began to attend some of the dances that were held at Russ Hall in their Helsinki neighborhood. At Mary's urging, she went to see a couple of her old girlfriends to find out what to wear to the dances. They were pleased that Hilda would once again be a part of the social life they so enjoyed. The girls would get together a couple of nights before the weekly dance and spend hours experimenting with face makeup and trying on each other's clothes. These activities were almost as much fun as going to the dance itself.

Determined to stay true to Albin, Hilda dressed as conservatively as she could so as not to attract too much attention from the boys. But she forgot to tell the boys they weren't supposed to notice her. There was a crowd of young men around Hilda from the minute she entered the hall.

Hilda's dress was one she made in her spare time at home. It was the plainest frock in her closet, a print covered with tiny forget-me-not flowers on a white background. It wasn't the dress that attracted young men like bees to a field of flowers, but what was obviously a womanly shape beneath the cloth.

Hilda, with her full figure and tiny waist, didn't realize that her conservative dress was a poor camouflage. When one of the men asked Hilda to dance, she declined. There was something about him that she didn't like. For one thing, he was too tall, so unlike Albin who was short. And he had no bulging muscles like Albin. Then she thought, "Why am I looking for a replacement for Albin? He will send for me some day soon now and I'll have the genuine article."

So she changed her mind and told the tall, slender Swede she would dance with him after all. From then on, it was one dance after another and pretty soon all of the men in the hall had at least one dance with the ravishing Hilda.

The Swede asked her, "Where have you been hiding? I thought I knew all the beautiful women in Helsinki, but this is the first time I have seen you here."

Hilda replied, "I am betrothed to a man who is in America right now. He will be sending for me soon. I haven't been around, you see, but decided to come out with my friends for a little fun. All I have is my fiancé's many letters to read," she lied.

The Swede replied, "I can understand that and your true love is very lucky to have you as his woman. But dancing is just a lot of fun and I hope you will continue to come to the dances anyway. You can stay true to your man and still enjoy your life. I'm Sven Guddal. I already know who you are, Hilda."

Hilda blushed. "This man is right", she decided, "and he seems so nice. What can it hurt to dance with the other young men in town? I will take his advice."

Hilda began to take care with her wardrobe. She made a few more dresses that would look great on the dance floor. While she sewed, she imagined herself waltzing gracefully in her beautiful royal blue dress to the lilting melody of the Varsouvienne.

ALBIN'S LETTERS

Chapter 11

When Albin got off the train in the huge railroad yards in Chicago he was amazed at how big everything was. And how dirty. It was almost two years since he had left Finland, but he remembered the quiet streets and tidy villages of his homeland as he picked his way through the trash of the rail yards until he saw a sign in English in a second floor window that he could read: "Room for Rent". Albin hoped he had enough to pay the first month's rent as he knocked on the shabby looking front door.

A heavy-set woman with bright red lipstick and a cigarette dangling from her mouth opened the door. She took a look at Albin and said, "We don't take little boys here," and started to shut the door.

He stopped her from closing the door with his arm, stuck out his chin as far as it would go and said, "I am not a boy, I am a man. I am short is all, but I can assure you I am old enough to be here."

She took another look and through the smoke she said, "Well, I guess you are. I can see the hair on your face so you must shave. Okay, what do you want?"

"I saw the sign. I need a place to live."

"Oh", the woman said,"I forgot that was up there. Yeah, I guess it isn't rented yet. Come in, honey, and I'll show it to you."

Albin wasn't sure he wanted to see it after walking through the entry way. The place was extremely dirty and there were a few women lounging around on cots and overstuffed chairs in various stages of undress. He followed the large woman up the stairs that creaked underfoot. He imagined the stairs crumbling underfoot when he came back down.

The woman led him down a dark hallway with many doors. He could hear talking and music from behind some of them, and a woman was singing behind one.

"People in Chicago don't seem to take much pride in how their residences appear to strangers," Albin thought. In Finland and the other Scandinavian countries, cleanliness is uppermost in the minds of its citizens. If you aren't clean, you are either a criminal or insane. These floors and steps would be swept and scrubbed clean if the building were in Helsinki.

An awful stench hit his nostrils as they walked through the building. It smelled like a combination of urine, whiskey and cheap perfume. Somebody at least tried to eliminate the odor by spraying perfume about. "It isn't working," thought Albin.

The woman stopped at a door and knocked. No reply. She knocked again. Stephanie, you in there? I have some guy who wants to rent the room. You have to clear out."

Pretty soon Stephanie opened the door a crack and a raspy voice said, "Tell him to come back later. I got somebody in here who's going to buy me a mink stole."

"Sorry, Steph. You have to get out now. And take the big spender with you."

"Aw, Liz, honey, you know I can't get myself together that fast. Give me about 15 minutes. Please!" the voice said.

So, "Liz-honey" looked at Albin and said, "C'mon down to the kitchen and I'll pour you a cup of coffee while the little lady makes herself ready.

Off they went, back down the treacherous

stairway. Albin was surprised to see that the kitchen was clean. It even smelled good, with freshly made coffee and the scent of apples and cinnamon wafting from a pie that was set to cool on the counter.

Liz waved Albin to a chair at the kitchen table, but as soon as he was seated he jumped up again as a cockroach crossed the table right in front of him.

"Damn roaches," Liz said as she smacked the critter with her hand. A loud crunch told Albin that it was dead. She swept it off the table and with the same hand poured Albin a cup of coffee.

The kitchen was painted a dark green that he later learned it was called "gas house green". He made a mental note to look into that designation. A single bulb hung from the ceiling, a spare tribute to Thomas Edison.

Albin took a sip of the coffee and was grateful for the kindness his soon-to-be landlady had already shown him.

He hadn't eaten in two days and when his stomach grumbled, Liz said, "That apple pie will be cool enough to eat in a minute."

"And where might you be from, lad?" she asked.

"I'm sorry, I should introduce myself", Albin said in broken English. "I'm Albin Putkonen, from Finland. I just (he pronounced it "yust") come in this morning on train from Oregon.

"I'm still learning speak English," he explained.

"And yer doin' good!" Liz said. "We're all from someplace else, Dearie, unless you're an Indian...

"Myself came from Ireland a couple of years ago," she added. "And pray what do you plan to do in this big city?"

"I have been working in logging camps and learned to cook. But also entertain as wrestler. My real job in old country was woodwork, making cabinets," Albin told the lady as she got up from the table and began to serve the pie. His mouth watered at the wonderful smell.

"Here ya go." Liz lifted a large slice onto on an almost clean plate and gave him a fork.

Albin didn't want to appear too ravenous, but he couldn't help himself as he downed the pie in almost one bite.

"Oh, darlin', ya didn't have to wolf it. I was goin' to put a spot of cream on it." She took the plate and refilled it with a larger slice of the pie and poured a thick dollop of rich, heavy cream over the top of the second slice, and refilled his coffee cup.

For the second time since arriving in the United States Albin felt as though the angels were near him. The first was the railroad stop in Kansas.

He looked at Liz and said, "That was good. Thank you very much," and smiled the biggest smile he could muster just before he fell asleep in the chair.

"Oh, you poor dear," Liz said softly. Albin must have slept an hour before waking to see Liz and another younger woman standing on the other side of the table looking at him.

"I'm sorry! I fall asleep!" an embarrassed Albin told the women.

"Well, you must have been very tired and after eating the warm pie. It is natural to fall asleep. I guess you haven't eaten anything solid in awhile," Liz said.

Albin decided then and there that no matter how dirty his new surroundings, living in this place would not be all that bad.

He followed Liz back upstairs to the little room Stephanie had recently vacated and checked it out.

He then turned to Liz and asked, "How much?"

"A dollar a week," Liz said, "but if you can't afford to pay until you find a job we'll just run a tab."

Albin was sure this would be a good arrangement. He settled in, tested the bed springs and in a few minutes he was again sound asleep.

ALBIN'S LETTERS

Chapter 12

Hilda awoke to the sounds of birds singing outside her window. The sun was already streaming in and making long shadows on the walls.

"Oh my, I have overslept. John will be furious!" she said aloud as she ran to her closet and grabbed her robe to wear down to breakfast.

She bumped into her sister-in-law as she opened her door. "Oh, I'm sorry, Mary. I rarely oversleep. John will kill me for sure!"

Mary shushed her. "I was just coming to see if you were all right. John had a meeting to attend early this morning so he isn't here. Come, Hilda. I have pancakes and maple syrup for your breakfast. I have kept breakfast warm for you."

Hilda was grateful for Mary's kindness. She always came to her defense when John was angry with her. Hilda always felt comfortable with Mary. She loved her almost as much as she had her own mother.

Mary was short, like all of the women in her family, like Hilda, who always wished she could have been taller. She figured if she were tall like her brother, John, he wouldn't pick on her so much.

Mary, following in the tradition of all the Swedish women of her day, wore her hair in a long braid, wound around in a bun in the back of her head. Hilda would wear her hair in the same style after she married. Until then, she preferred to wear it in long curls, or in braids that hung down her back tied with ribbons on the ends.

Hilda, also like the other women, was quiet, reserved and well read. It was required of all the Sjostedt children that they read the entire works of Shakespeare before they finished school. They also were taught economics and calculus and most of them could play at least one musical instrument before the age of 12.

Hilda's mother, who remained in Sweden with her husband, was not only an accomplished pianist she also painted the most beautiful landscapes in oils. The entire family was proficient at some form of performing and visual arts. Hilda expressed her creativity in sewing exquisite garments from delicate fabrics. Her musical talents were confined to singing. She was blessed with a clear and strong contralto voice.

Since she was about eight years old, Hilda sang in the church choir. John, a member of the Lutheran Church of Finland, insisted that she attend church every Sunday and that she participate in all aspects of the church community. Besides the choir, Hilda was required to teach Sunday school for the younger children after she had been instructed in the catechism and confirmed when she was twelve years old.

Hilda loved being involved with her church. She enjoyed all of the church's activities and felt comforted after attending services and participating with other church members at the myriad of activities during the week.

Hilda never missed a Sunday service except for the time she spent with Albin in Mikkeli. But she said her prayers every night, and told Albin that once they were married, they would not miss a Sunday at church.

Albin agreed to this, but in retrospect he may have been talking in the heat of passion when he might have agreed to almost anything.

Hilda and her sister-in-law ate breakfast in

silence. Neither one mentioned the absence of John.

Hilda sighed, "I don't know what I am going to do if I don't hear from my Albin pretty soon."

Mary sipped her hot coffee through a sugar cube from a saucer as always. She didn't speak right away. Then she said, "You know, Hilda, your brother and I want what is best for you. Maybe pinning your hopes on Albin after all these months is not a good idea. Maybe Albin has found someone else by now. You could get used to another man, too."

Hilda threw down her napkin and she got up so quickly she almost knocked over the dishes on the table. "Don't say that, Mary! Don't tell me Albin has found another woman! He promised me he would send for me!" Hilda began to cry.

Mary felt helpless when Hilda cried. She didn't know how to console her sister-in-law in this situation. She knew John was withholding Albin's letters, but he had forbidden her to tell Hilda. All she could do was pat Hilda's back and lie, "It will be all right, you'll see." But she stopped short of repeating what she'd said about Hilda getting used to another man. That would be mean.

Eventually Hilda pulled herself together and

went off to work. This day would be especially difficult for her. One of the girls she was particularly fond of was leaving to be married and her friends were throwing her a surprise party after work.

Each time a woman in the neighborhood or at work got married, Hilda became sad and moped around for days. "When will it be my turn?" Hilda asked herself at every wedding.

A melancholy Hilda left work without attending the party and headed for the city park. She sat on a bench and watched the small children at play. Nannies sat nearby, talking about how bright their charges were, and how generous the parents were in letting them watch their children, day and night.

Nannies held a special place in the community. Most were well paid because usually both mothers and fathers were employed at the factory. John saw to it that parents with young children had an extra amount of cash in their pay envelopes each week.

Hilda wondered if she should apply for a nanny position. She could do the job easily and it would at least keep her occupied longer hours thereby spending more time away from her brother who often criticized how she spent her time.

She went up to one of the nannies and introduced herself, then asked the young woman if she knew of any parents in need of someone to care for their children.

The woman introduced herself as Helga Halonen and said, "As a matter of fact, I do. The sister of the woman I work for has just gone to work at the factory. She needs a nanny. Tell me your name and I will have her come to see you."

Hilda gave the woman her address and thanked her, then headed home. "Well, just like that! I will change my career and maybe even learn how to be a good mother to Albin's children!"

She was buoyant when she went into John's house a few minutes later and made her announcement.

Mary was delighted and hugged Hilda. John was surly and didn't try to hide his feelings.

"Hmph! What kind of nonsense is that! Anybody can take care of children. Working in a factory is a much more honorable pursuit. Forget it, Hilda. You are chasing rainbows," he added as he went back to drinking his before-dinner Scotch.

"Why does he always put me down?" Hilda

asked Mary when they were out of earshot of John. "No matter what I want to do, especially if he thinks it will make me happy, it's not good enough for him."

She went into the kitchen and began to set the table for dinner. "I'll do what I want and work where I want," she said to Mary. "My brother has no idea how stubborn I can be." She swished her long skirt as she flounced up the stairs to her room to wait until Mary called her for supper.

It wasn't until the following day, after supper, that a young matron knocked on the Sarvimaara's front door.

"My name is Tarja Paavinen and I wish to speak to Hilda."

"I am Hilda," she replied.

"Helga told me you are looking for a nanny position," Tarja said.

"I am, yes." As they began to talk, there was an instant bond between the two women. Hilda went with Tarja to her apartment, which was only a couple of blocks away, to meet her small children. Martti was a sturdy little blond boy of six, and her daughter Esteri, five, was dark-haired and delicate as a China doll. She was surprised to learn that Tarja was a widow at such a young age. Tarja explained, "My husband was killed in an accident at the factory."

Hilda was horrified, "I am so sorry," she said. "So you are also employed at the factory?" Hilda asked.

"I just went to work there after my husband was killed. We were making it all right with just one paycheck, but now I must work. The factory had no compensation for me because my Eero hadn't worked there long enough to qualify."

Hilda wondered how this could be. She always thought her brother was generous to his workers, especially if they were hurt at work. In this case, a widow lost everything when she lost her husband to an accident while working for John Sarvimaara.

Hilda promised herself she would ask John about this injustice the next time she had a chance to talk to him.

She got acquainted with the children at that first meeting and made arrangements to be there in the morning to fix their breakfast and get them dressed for the day.

Chapter 13

Hilda was ecstatic to begin working as the Paavinen children's nanny. Being a nanny was the next best thing to being a mother, Hilda figured. She would make sure that Tarja would not be sorry for hiring her.

She kept the house clean for the family, and if Tarja was too tired after working all day at the factory Hilda would stay long enough to ready the children for bed.

"Where did I find such an angel," Tarja told Hilda after the first week was over. "You are so kind to the children and now you are even cleaning for me and putting the children to bed. I only wish I could pay you what you are truly worth."

Hilda took Tarja's hands into hers and said, "You are like a sister to me, Tarja. And you have suffered so much for one so young. I can't imagine what it would be like to lose a loving husband and father. You are the remarkable one. You are the angel here."

Tarja gave Hilda a hug and said, "Someday you

will get your just reward. It may be when you get to heaven. I will hate to lose you, Hilda, but I know you will have Albin with you very soon."

She sounded sincere when she talked about Albin, but she had already heard the women at the factory say that Albin hadn't written to Hilda in over a year. "There will be no marriage to Albin, I'm afraid," she thought. "I am so sad for her."

About two weeks after Hilda went to work for Tarja, she heard about a dance to be held at the Russo-Finn Hall downtown. The building used to be called Swede Hall, but the name had recently been changed to reflect the current Russian rule.

Hilda decided she needed a little dancing to lift her spirits, so she finished the blue dress she'd been sewing for the past month and hoped the band would play a Varsouvienne waltz.

She stepped inside the door and the first person she saw was Sven Guddal, the lanky Swede who had flirted with her at the last dance.

Sven's eyes lit up and he gave Hilda a dazzling smile to match. He really was a handsome man, Hilda admitted to herself. His blond hair, almost white, was cropped short, but a large pompadour on top made him appear even taller. Bright blue eyes with long blond eyelashes were his most attractive feature. His pale skin turned bright pink when he blushed, as he was doing now at the sight of the lovely Hilda. He wasn't as muscular as Albin, Hilda noticed, but he had a nice physique for one whose only exercise she knew about first-hand was dancing and, according to newspaper articles, riding horses and playing polo. She was also sure he did a lot of skiing in the winter months. She wondered if he also swam in a cold lake after bathing in the sauna.

Sven was, Hilda learned, related to Swedish aristocracy and a very wealthy man in his own right. She heard he was even wealthier than John, if that were possible.

Hilda danced almost every dance with Sven and was beginning to feel a little self conscious about tying up the handsome Swede's time on the dance floor. She was sure there were other women there who would have enjoyed dancing with him.

But he was a good dancer and Hilda liked the way he lifted her off her feet as they danced a lively Swedish polka.

Then the orchestra began to play the slow and

stately strains of the waltz for which Hilda had made the blue gown: The Varsouvienne.

They were alone on the floor all through the dance. Couples had begun to dance but as Sven and Hilda dipped and twirled to the music everyone had drawn back to the outside of the floor leaving the handsome couple in the center. When the music ended, all of the others applauded. Hilda was embarrassed at the attention and was breathless, not just at the physical accomplishment, but at the pure enjoyment of this most graceful dancer.

They sat out the next dance and then Sven asked Hilda if she would like to step outside for a breath of fresh air. They found a glider swing and sat down. Hilda didn't know how to react when Sven held up her chin and kissed her, ever so lightly, on the mouth. She enjoyed that kiss and then immediately felt guilty.

"Oh, Sven," Hilda gasped. "You know I am engaged to marry Albin! I shouldn't have let you kiss me!"

Without a word Sven kissed her again, this time longer and more deeply. Hilda began to feel that familiar warm thrill inside.

Suddenly, she jumped up and cried, "No, Sven, we mustn't! It is wrong!" She gathered up her long skirt and made a dash for home.

As she flew into the house Mary asked, "What's wrong, girl? You look as if you've seen a ghost!"

"Oh, Mary, I have done a dreadful thing! I let a boy kiss me on the mouth. Oh, what will Albin say when he finds out!"

"Ah, Hilda, don't be silly. So you let a boy kiss you, so what? Albin has been gone a long time. It is natural for you to have desires. A woman needs to be loved and since Albin may never be seen by any of us again, what is the harm in finding a little pleasure?"

Hilda didn't want to hear that. She didn't want to hear that she may never see Albin again. She would die an old maid first.

She went to her room and threw herself down on her bed. This was the first time Hilda would fall asleep without making an entry in her journal, telling Albin how much she loved him and how much she wanted to be with him. She cried softly as she remembered Mary's words, "It is natural for you to have desires."

Her fitful sleep was interrupted by several dreams, all of which were of Albin: Albin swimming away from the beach, Albin running up a mountain, Albin riding a horse into the meadow…

"Albin," she cried in her sleep. Mary could hear her and cried along with her.

Chapter 14

Albin learned to get around Chicago and found out where all of the best bars were the first night. He went in for a beer, which cost him a nickel. Pretty steep, he thought. But he had some money left over from his last wrestling match, so he had a couple more drinks.

A young Irishman sitting near him at the bar turned to Albin and asked, "So where do ye hail from, lad?"

Albin told him "Finland."

"And wot be yer name?" asked the Irishman.

"Albin Putkonen, sir."

"If ye leave out the 'Put' you could be an Irish lad named 'Conan'," he said with mock seriousness. Then he laughed heartily.

Albin didn't take offense at this. He had heard other Finns express anger when Americans and Canadians made fun of their Finnish names. The fights that followed weren't worth it.

He laughed along with the Irishman. "And wot be yer name," he mimicked the Irishman.

"Clancy. Clancy O'Toole, the best rassler this side o' the Atlantic Ocean."

Albin couldn't believe his ears. This man was a wrestler like him. But maybe not just like him. He sized him up and determined that this slightly built lad, although taller than Albin, might be an easy win.

He asked the man, "And where do you do your rasslin'?"

"Oh, we have a hall where lots o' at'letic events take place. It's the union hall, but they rent it out for rasslin' and boxin' matches. A lotta bettin' takes place and yer can make a pretty penny if yer wins," Clancy added.

Albin rubbed his stubble and asked, "Where do ya sign up?"

Clancy looked at the diminutive Finn and said, "Oh, ya don't wanna get yerself kilt, do ya? The rasslers are big. Most of 'em bigger'n me."

Albin said, "I've done some wrestling and I think I'm pretty good."

Clancy threw his head back and roared. When he finished laughing he could hardly get his breath. "Yer a spunky one, ye are, I'll give yer that. But if ye really wanna try, there's a crowd gonna be at the hall tonight. I kin getcha a spot on the program, and ye'll have to pay an entry fee of a buck-fifty. Do ye have any shorts and wrestlin' shoes?"

Albin told Clancy he did indeed have a wrestling costume and the proper shoes. He asked where he should pay his buck-fifty.

Clancy looked at Albin with more respect and told him to walk with him over to the hall. He would help him get signed up.

Off they went in the direction of the union hall. After Albin paid the fee to wrestle in the large cavernous building, he returned to his room at the boarding house and retrieved his bag containing the colorful clothes and shoes he wore when he competed in wrestling matches. When Albin went back to the hall a noisy crowd had already gathered around the large mat on the floor. A couple of men stepped up the center of the mat and a referee waved his arm to signal the start of the match. It only took a few minutes when one of them pinned his opponent and the first match was over.

Albin was listed second on the bill so he quickly changed from his street clothes and into his costume and was ready to go to work. He was surprised to see his opponent was Clancy! When Albin walked out on the mat the crowd began to laugh uproariously. They were pointing at Albin. He asked Clancy what they were laughing at.

Clancy could hardly contain himself he was laughing so hard. "It's yer get-up, Finn. These guys have never seen such a fancy outfit on a rassler before!"

Albin looked down at his red silk knee length shorts, bright blue knee socks, and the brightly colored yellow print sash tied around his waist, and wondered why they would laugh at such an elegant costume.

Just then Clancy grabbed Albin and threw him to the mat. The ref counted to three as Clancy pinned him. It was over in 30 seconds.

"Aw, ye shouldn't feel so bad, Finn," Clancy told the defeated Albin. "Ye will have a chance to get back at me tomorrow night. There's another match!"

"Yeah," Albin said, "but I'm gettin' short of

cash and at this rate I'll be too broke to buy groceries by the end of the week."

"I can lend ye a five spot," Clancy said. "Ye can pay me back on payday."

"That would be okay if I had a payday comin," Albin said. "I don't have a job yet."

"So wot kind of work do ye do?"

"I can cook and make copper pots. I was also pretty good at making furniture," Albin told him.

"They need a cook over at the Bull and Bash," Clancy told him. "C'mon, I'll take ye over and introduce ye to Big John. He's the bloke wot owns the place and if ye really can cook, ye'll have a job fer life."

And so it happened that Big John was Swedish. In Sweden his name was spelled Jan and was pronounced "Yon". Albin quickly connected with the big boisterous "Yon" when he pronounced his name as Albin knew it should be spoken.

Albin was sure he could get along with this big Swede. And he knew he could cook circles around any chef in the area, especially if Scandinavian dishes were popular.

Big John took to the Finn-boy right away. "Yah got a yob if yah can make Swedish meatballs. Dat's wot all da guys like around here, ya sure! Grab an apron, Cookie, and let's make supper."

* * *

Hilda was really enjoying her new job as nanny and the kids loved her from the first day. She liked to tell them stories as they sat on her lap in the kitchen. Mary came over to visit Hilda on her second day and adored those little ones as well.

"They are so well-behaved," Mary said, "and such beautiful children. Their snow white hair reminds me of you when you were a child, Hilda. I used to love to make long curls in your hair when you got dressed in the morning before going to school. You didn't like to have your hair brushed, but we managed to get through each morning with the long curls."

"I look forward to your having daughters of your own, Hilda. You will make a wonderful mother some day. Maybe being a nanny was meant to be. It is good training for the day when you become a Mama."

As the children played with their little toys,

Hilda and Mary had a chance to talk. "You know, Mary, you might be right," mused Hilda. "Albin may have found another woman over there. It's been a long time since we were together and he's a very romantic guy. I wouldn't stand in his way if he wanted to get on with his life. It's been two years since we saw each other." But she said it as if it couldn't possibly be true.

"Anyway," Hilda continued, "I have made a decision. I will go out with Sven if he still wants me to. I wasn't very nice to him last week at the dance."

"Oh, Hilda," Mary exclaimed. "That's a very mature decision!"

"If I can get in touch with Sven's parents, John and I might make an arrangement for marriage between these two," Mary thought to herself.

Out loud, she said, "I have met Sven and I know his parents have a very good reputation around town." She didn't add: "And they're very rich!"

"Then it's settled," Mary said.

"What's settled, Mary?"

"Oh—it's settled that you will date Sven," Mary quickly recovered. She didn't want to give Hilda the impression that Sven's parents' money was the motivation for her enthusiasm.

Hilda went home that night and wrote in her journal: "My darling Albin, I don't know what to think since I have not heard from you in two years.

"My heart aches to tell you, my dear Albin, I have decided to take a lover. He is a nice Swedish boy and would surely make a good husband.

"You would be my first choice, of course. But you are not here, Albin. I have to get on with my life and you must get on with yours.

"I have an idea that you already have a new life. You must have forgotten me by now. I have no idea where you are, if you are sick or well… or if you are dead or alive.

"I think this is for the best right now."

Hilda closed the journal and put it away in the bottom of a drawer she rarely went through, one filled with mementos and letters from old school friends and old family pictures. She closed the drawer and it was like closing a chapter in her life.

"Rest in peace, Albin," she said aloud softly.

Then Hilda went to sleep without shedding a tear. Nor did she have any more wild dreams about Albin. Peace.

ALBIN'S LETTERS

Chapter 15

A healthy new respect for the sport of wrestling overtook Albin as he suffered his fourth night of defeat on the union hall mats. He had not come close to beating Clancy, but he hadn't given up. Not yet.

A new brute entered the ring and challenged Clancy. Carl Hogstrom was a big Swedish fellow who had come to America about a year before Albin. He struck up a conversation with Albin on his first night when Clancy had floored him in seconds. Carl was pinned in about six seconds, a record so far that month. He came off the mat and sat on a bench next to Albin.

They talked as they watched Clancy go on to pin three more husky men. Albin told him about his arrival in New York Harbor and related the scare he got when the immigration officials said he may have to return to Finland.

Hogstrom rolled his eyes when Albin came to the story of being rescued by the logging boss, Ole Johanson. "That's my Uncle Ole! I worked with him for awhile when I came over, but I didn't care for that life. I wanted to be in a big city, not a big forest, so I quit when we got to Lake Superior where there was a boat sailing down to Lake Michigan and headed for Chicago."

Hogstrom had worked at a foundry in Stockholm and knew he wanted to do something with iron, the metal that fascinated him. He was drawn to Chicago because he had heard it was the hub of the country's railroad system. The fact that iron was vital to the development and maintenance of railroads across the country further galvanized his belief that this is where he wanted to be.

Carl's skills in iron-working had brought him back to his original occupation, forging iron at a foundry. So Hogstrom spent his working days in front of a blast furnace at the foundry and his nights drinking whiskey and wrestling punks at the union hall.

Albin liked the big Swede and being single like him further bonded their friendship. Albin also learned that Carl was saving up his money to send for his sweetheart who was still in Sweden. They already had much in common.

When Carl found out Albin was the cook at

the Bull and Bash, that became his regular mealtime hang out. The two became good friends.

One night when Albin was leaving the union hall, a couple of men were blocking his exit. Albin said, "Pardon me, sirs, but I am trying to pass through here."

One of the men put his hand on Albin's shoulders and said, "Don't you recognize us, Albin?"

Albin looked a little closer and it finally sunk in. There, blocking his exit, were his old Finnish friends who left Sointula when he was ill with scarlet fever. Esko Kekkonen and the Tynjala brothers, friends he had lived with in Helsinki and who traveled with him all across Canada working the logging camps, had found him in Chicago.

He hugged the two men and said, "My God! How did you ever find me?"

Esko said, "Well, we knew you were coming to Chicago eventually. We visited Sointula one last time and they told us you had taken off for Oregon. We found out also that Gustav had married that woman, Lempe, who showed us around when we got there. We were told she had nursed the two of you back to health and that she and Gus fell in love. Guess she must have liked what she saw when she gave you guys a bath. Well, Gus, anyway!" he laughed.

"You left a trail," Esko continued. "We heard about how that crook in Portland robbed you of your wrestling money. And then we lost track of where you went after that. Where did you go, anyway?"

Albin related the story of how he got on a freight train headed for Chicago after Pulaski threatened to kill him. He told them about the trouble he had before the train got to Kansas and how he came to lose his pants and shoes, and then about finding a friendly bunch of fellows who restored his hope since coming to America.

"C'mon, you guys. I am a cook at a diner close by. I can buy your dinner," and the foursome left for the Bull and Bash, hashing over what they had been doing all this time.

Over dinner the Finns decided that they might get better jobs if they could speak and write the English language. Albin heard about a college in Indiana about 45 miles from Chicago. They agreed this was something they should do. Albin asked his boss about getting a couple of weeks off. Big John said it would be no problem with the cooking at the restaurant. He could handle it until Albin returned.

The next day Albin collected his paycheck and the Finns took off for Valparaiso College to learn how to speak English like an American. Well almost. After they returned, they learned their Scandinavian accent would probably always be with them.

Albin wasn't at all on Hilda's mind for the next week as she cared for Tarja's children. When she wasn't occupied with fixing meals for the little ones and Tarja, and washing and ironing clothes for the family she thought of what she would wear to the next dance.

She looked at her wardrobe and decided she needed to take some fabric and her little charges over to the Paavinen house and make a dress while the children took their naps. She chose an elegant brown chiffon with a brown satin lining with a scoop-necked frock. She decided this was the most sophisticated dress in her closet. She would certainly attract attention when she walked into the hall Friday evening.

Hilda was right. There wasn't a girl or woman there who could even come close to the petite Hilda

Sjostedt in her beautiful new creation.

Sven was, of course, infatuated from the first moment he saw her.

Sven, for all his sophistication and wealth, was actually a shy person. Hilda noticed at once how reserved he had been at that first dance. Hilda, always a champion of the underdog, didn't want to hurt his feelings and she was afraid she had when she spurned him at the last dance and told him she was spoken for.

Sven didn't want to steal her away from Albin, but he couldn't help but feel Hilda wasn't all that convinced that she would ever see Albin again.

After growing up in a world of strict adherence to what was considered "proper" in polite society, Sven had an urge to get out of this sheltered and stifling environment to see what the rest of the world was like. That's when he started attending the dances. He met a few other attractive Finnish girls from the neighborhood, but no girl made him feel like Hilda did.

From the moment he saw her he wanted to have her. He dreamed of taking her to his beautiful secluded garden and seducing her on the lush grass, surrounded by lavender and fragrant rose bushes. He wanted Hilda for his own, to bear his children, to live with him in the cottage his family had built for him and his bride.

Sven had shown an interest in politics at an early age and his tutors had related this to his parents. From then on they instructed the tutors to groom their only son for a seat in parliament. Surely he would shine in a high position in the country's government one day. They wanted him to be up to the task when that time came.

Sven was a studious fellow, but he also liked to dance and have fun. He hid from his parents the fact that he was sweet on a girl he had met at the dances. He also hid from them his addiction to alcohol, which he pilfered from the house cellar when his parents and the servants weren't around.

Hilda's brother John wasted no time when he heard the name Sven Guddal from his wife as the man who was interested in his sister.

"Mary!" he shouted. "This is an answer to a prayer! This man is from a very wealthy family and would make a superb husband for Hilda!"

John went to his desk and began drafting a

letter to Sven Guddal's parents, the August Guddals. He wrote that he would reluctantly give his niece's hand in marriage if the dowry would be sufficient enough. He wrote down a large sum for the Guddals to consider.

He wrote of the many talents and accomplishments of Hilda and challenged them to find another woman of such high caliber anywhere in Helsinki.

John posted the letter immediately. Then he told Mary what he had done.

"Oh, John, how can you be so indelicate! You never talked to Hilda about this. It must be her decision to make."

"Rubbish," John shouted at Mary just as Hilda walked through the front door.

She heard the shouting coming from the other room and, not caring to get between Mary and John no matter what they were sparring about this time, Hilda went to her room and closed the door.

Chapter 16

Life in Chicago after the turn of the century was what Albin described in his letters to Hilda as "exhilarating. When you see all of the energy of the people who live here you will be excited, too.

"There are so many things going on at once. There are large building projects taking place all over the city. Much of it was ruined in 1871 during a big fire, but all that has been cleaned up and now construction of new buildings is going on. So many new buildings!

"I am happy with my job as a cook in a small restaurant for now, but I will find something more suitable before you come, dear Hilda. I signed up with a company that makes copper boilers for heating large buildings, but I must first join a union so I am saving up for that. Everything costs so much, I can't seem to save money out of my paychecks for all of it.

"But soon I will have enough to send to you, Hilda, so you can book passage on a boat and come join me."

Albin now had a real address at the boarding

house and expected any day to receive a letter from Hilda. He waited several months with no letter in his mailbox.

Meanwhile, there was a lot for him to do while he waited. He still entered the wrestling matches when he had enough time off from work. One day Clancy went to him at the restaurant and said, "Hey, Albin, some of us are going up to Milwaukee for the weekend. There's a big pavilion up there and many wrestlers are just waiting to get pinned by us. Come along. I think they have some pretty big purses and we can make a lot of money."

Albin wasn't sure how much to believe when Clancy was doing the talking. But he didn't have anything better to do so he packed a small bag and brought along his wrestling costume, just in case.

Clancy and Albin and two other men from the neighborhood went down to the railroad station and paid for tickets to Milwaukee. When they arrived, the young men asked directions to the arena when they got there and when they found out it was only a few long blocks away, they decided to walk.

A saloon was conveniently located right next door to the arena so the men decided to have a pint before going in to look over the competition. Albin sat up to the bar and jokingly said, "We've come to find your best wrestlers and destroy them."

The bartender reached across the bar and grabbed Albin's collar and said, "You'd better watch your mouth, stranger. There are a lot of us and only a few of you."

He let go of Albin after the warning, but didn't take his eyes off of him. A couple of the bar regulars sat up straight and one of them said, "Did I hear somebody from out of town challenge our guys? I don't think these blokes look so tough." The fight was on.

One of them grabbed Clancy and sucker punched him. Another got hold of Albin and unceremoniously threw him across the room. Albin crashed through several tables and chairs and landed in a heap by the front window of the saloon. The other two Chicago wrestlers were outnumbered by the Milwaukee bunch.

The cops came and quickly broke up the fight. The only one really hurt was Albin who was taken to the nearest hospital to get stitched up.

More embarrassed than physically hurt, Albin

told Clancy when he got out of the hospital, "I don't think we were supposed to come up here, Clancy. Maybe we'd better skip the wrestling on this trip." They left on the next train going south.

Back in Chicago, they decided that people in Milwaukee had no sense of humor and they'd be better off without them. "I think that bartender took my remarks the wrong way," Albin said. The others solemnly agreed.

"Ya," Clancy said, "We could have stayed in Chicago to get the crap beat out of us."

There would be no more leaving town to find wrestling partners.

"Dear Hilda, well, I did a stupid thing and want you to hear about it from me before you get to America. There's a town near Chicago called Milwaukee…"

Chapter 17

Hilda checked to make sure her dress and hair were perfect before she left her bedroom. She was nervous about meeting Marta and Luke Guddal, Sven's parents. She was surprised at how quickly things were going since her brother wrote to the Guddals and made arrangements for the families to get together so they could plan for Hilda's and Sven's future.

Hilda never thought she would actually go through with marrying Sven, but at the last dance he took her outside again and this time he got on his knees and asked her to marry him.

This took her by surprise even though she half expected it to happen. Just not in such a short amount of time. "What will happen if I hear from Albin? Then what?"

Hilda didn't say yes right away. "If I don't hear from Albin before the wedding, I'll marry you." Hilda didn't really expect to hear from Albin after all this time.

She put him out of her mind for the time being. She couldn't go through with this evening's planned dinner with Sven's parents if she started thinking about Albin.

She walked downstairs where John and Mary were waiting, dressed in their finest clothes. Mary looked so grand in a dark green, satin brocade frock. John was in a black cutaway tuxedo with black bow tie and ruffled white shirt. She had never been to a formal event with her brother and sister-in-law and was pleasantly surprised at how nice they looked tonight.

Hilda looked especially elegant in the blue gown she had made especially for the dance a few weeks ago when Sven had stolen a kiss outside the hall. Even John smiled when she descended the stairway. "You look lovely, Hilda," he said. Hilda gasped slightly. It was the first time John had ever made a remark about her appearance, except about a year ago when he told her the dress she wore showed too much décolleté. Tonight was different. He wanted her to be a good catch for Sven; the more décolleté the better.

When Hilda was helped by a butler from the horse-drawn carriage her heart went into a tailspin. "If I marry Sven will we have butlers and maids to do our bidding? Will we have a cook to prepare our food? This would be wonderful," Hilda thought. Although Hilda had been well trained in all of the other domestic arts, cooking never came easy to her. Her brother would often remark when Hilda helped Mary in the kitchen: "I see we are having another burnt dinner tonight."

Hilda couldn't cook anything that didn't come out overcooked. She became known in her family for batches of burnt biscuits. Even brewing coffee, something that was second nature to most Swedish women, was a disaster for Hilda.

John often said, "If Hilda is boiling water you have to watch she doesn't burn it."

The three were ushered through tall, elegantly hand-carved wooden doors into a large, two story high foyer. A huge bouquet of lavender and other garden flowers was arranged on a round table in the center of the big room. The lavender made the whole room come alive with its powerful scent.

The butler took their capes. She was surprised to see him drape them over the back of a chair near the front door. "With all this wealth they don't have a coat closet?" Hilda thought.

She wasn't allowed to dwell on this matter. Mr.

and Mrs. Guddal were striding from a large doorway toward them. Luke, Sven's father, put out his hand to John and said "Hello, I am Luke Guddal and this is my wife, Marta." As was the custom, all parties shook hands.

Standing there and feeling awkward at first, it was Marta who broke the silence: "Come along to the parlor. We can sit and have an aperitif before dinner."

As they entered the cozy parlor with many overstuffed chairs and divans even John was impressed. "What a lovely room," he exclaimed.

"Thank you, Mr. — may I call you John?"

"Of course, Luke. I think the occasion calls for first names."

"Marta has to take credit for all of the decorating in the house. She's the one with the artistic bent."

As they sat down, the same butler slid a tray of small glasses filled with a berry colored liqueur onto the cocktail table. Again, Hilda thought this was strange.

Just then Sven strode into the room, slightly

out of breath. "I'm sorry, Mama and Papa. I'm late because I had to brush Pauli when I was through riding her. Then I had to bathe, of course."

Hilda hoped Pauli was the name of his horse.

Sven came right over to the loveseat where Hilda was sitting and sat down beside her.

Then he quickly stood and said, "I beg your pardon. I have not met Mrs. Sarvimaara." He put out his hand to shake hers and she took it in both of hers. "I'm happy to meet you Sven. Please, call me Mary."

With all of the formalities taken care of, the rest of the afternoon was spent talking about politics, the fact that young men would soon have to serve in the military, and the moral decay since so many of the young people were engaging in wild sauna parties.

Hilda blushed. She wondered if the Guddals had heard about the parties in Mikkeli when she was there with Albin. She never told Sven about the brief period she and Albin lived with his sister, Olga. She never even told Mary who assumed that Albin's sister had a separate room for Hilda. Since Hilda never said otherwise, and it was doubtful that any of Albin's relatives or friends would come down here from Mikkeli and explain, she just let them think the best.

"I heard about the sauna parties," Hilda said. "How exciting!"

Sven said, "Oh, I don't know, Hilda. I hear that the sauna bath is quite healthful and invigorating."

Just then, a maid came into the room and announced, "Dinner is served."

Hilda breathed a sigh of relief. She didn't want to talk or hear about sauna bath parties anymore today, especially since that one small drink went to her head and she was known to talk too much when she was even a little tipsy.

They went to the dining room in couples, and Sven held out Hilda's chair for her. This was a first for Hilda who usually had to wrestle her own chair from under the table and seat herself. The room was another surprise. Unlike the parlor that had only family portraits on the walls, this hall had paintings by famous artists of the period. There must have been thirty in all. Hilda felt like she was in an art gallery with all of the masters' paintings hung strategically on the walls of this handsome room. She only recognized some of the more famous impressionists exhibited here, but she felt sure the other works were by equally important artists.

The table before them was in itself an artistic masterpiece, set with exquisite bone china, several crystal wineglasses at each setting and underneath it all expensive linen cloth. The fabric in the table cloth and napkins interested Hilda most since fabrics were what she worked with on a daily basis, making her own clothes and garments for Tarja's children.

The maid (followed by the butler) busied herself bringing out huge trays and tureens filled with food.

Hilda, who was used to rather plain cooking at her brother's home, couldn't identify what some of the dishes contained but enjoyed every bite of whatever it was, followed by some of the best wine she had ever tasted.

By the time they got to the dessert course, Hilda was well on her way to being drunk. Just as the plate filled with lingonberries and thick cream was in place her head drooped forward and her face came in contact with her dessert.

Mary and Marta quickly surrounded Hilda and carried her to the kitchen where they cleaned her up and sat her down at the kitchen table with a cup of strong Swedish coffee. The two women looked at one another, glum expressions on their faces, and Marta said, "The maid, Bess, has a room off the butler's pantry with a small bed. We can let Hilda sleep in there for an hour while we retire to the parlor for coffee."

Mary agreed it would be best. They tucked in Hilda and closed the door with instructions to Bess for her to not be disturbed.

Returning to the dining room just in time to see the men heading for the drawing room for their cigars and brandy, Marta said, "Let's you and I go to the parlor while they smoke. We need to talk."

"Hilda will be all right," she called to the men as they went into the other room, "She just needs to rest a little."

Sven, who had once seen Hilda after having a little too much to drink, was okay with it. John, who had never seen his sister drink at all, was mortified. "I don't think she's used to drinking wine," he told Luke. Luke just smiled as he lit up his cigar.

The two women sat down in the parlor where Bess served them coffee.

"I am embarrassed for Hilda," Mary said. "I

think this has been too much for her tonight. She has practically starved herself to get into that blue dress, yanno."

"She looks beautiful, Mary, and you shouldn't worry about her having a bit too much to drink. I have done the same thing on occasion," Marta admitted.

"So now we should talk about the wedding," and Marta brought out a small pad of paper and a writing quill with a vessel of ink. It was clear to Mary that Marta would be the designer of her sister-in-law's wedding. She didn't like it much, but after all, the Guddals were so wealthy it was natural that they would be in charge.

And so the plans for Sven and Hilda's wedding began.

ALBIN'S LETTERS

Chapter 18

If Albin was thinking about anything at the moment, it was certainly not about a wedding. At least not Hilda's wedding to somebody else.

Albin was just waking up the day after returning to Chicago from Milwaukee. As he rubbed his head, which felt like it was three times as big this morning, he thought to himself, "What was I thinking?"

He knew from experience it was never a good idea to broadcast your intent to pin an opponent to the mat. What possessed him to mouth off in that bar when they got to Milwaukee he didn't know. Boasting wasn't the best approach to challenging another wrestler.

He got up and splashed cold water on his face. He wondered what Hilda would think about him getting drunk and shooting off his mouth. He knew she wouldn't approve. She hardly drank any alcohol at all.

He went downstairs and knocked on Liz's door.

"Hello, Liz," Albin said to his landlady. "I have a splitting headache and wondered if you had any kind of medicine I could take for it."

Liz had all kinds of pill bottles in her kitchen cupboard, but nothing for a headache. "What you need is a steam bath and a Swedish massage."

Albin was open to anything that would make him feel better. "You don't have a sauna bath near here, do ya?"

Liz said, "A what?"

He realized there probably weren't enough Finns in Chicago yet to have established this old country custom and said, "Never mind. I'll explain it to you sometime. Just tell me where to go for the steam bath."

Liz directed him to an upstairs apartment in the next building and told him to ask for Big Ellie.

Big Ellie was a large, buxom woman with a thick blond braid wound around the top of her head. She had a cigar in her mouth when she answered the door.

"I hear you give a steam bath and a Swedish massage. I am in need of both, please," Albin tells the woman.

"Vell, hokay, little feller. You yust come on in

here and I'll give ya da full treatment!" Ellie roars.

Albin didn't know what "the full treatment" was but he was hurting so badly from getting beat up in Milwaukee and all the whisky he drank, he didn't care.

Big Ellie took him to a raised bed, more like a hospital cot, and told him to take off all his clothes and lie down.

Albin wasn't so sure he needed to remove his clothes, but he didn't want to argue with the large female with the big hands so he complied.

"Oh, my Got!" Ellie said. "Vere is da ape vot tried to eat you?"

"He didn't try to eat me, he just wanted to grind me up a little."

Big Ellie began working on Albin right away. She was busy working his shoulder muscles and then stopped. "No vay ve gonna do dis 'til you take a steam bath. You are 'vay too tense."

So she had him wrap a towel about his waist and led him down a hallway to the make shift steam room. Albin went inside and it was his turn to be surprised. This looked exactly like a sauna. It even had the small stove with the crib on top for the hot rocks and the kettle of water to pour on them.

He asked Ellie, "Did you build this sauna?"

"Yah shure! But da folks around here call it a steam bath so dat's vot it is."

Albin was so happy at the prospect of having a real sauna he forgot to ask where the snow was for afterwards. Ellie must have read his mind. She said, "Da only ting missing is da snow! Yah?"

"Yah," said Albin. "But I betcha got a cold shower instead."

"Yah, sure! Good guess, Finn."

Albin finally got through the sauna, shower and Ellie's pounding on his shoulders, back and legs, and he walked out of there feeling like soft butter. When he left her apartment, he paid her and gave her a generous tip. He said, "I'll be back!"

Back at the boarding house, Liz met him at the door. "Youse got company. In yer room," she said. "They can stay if they like but you have to get a mattress for them to sleep on and you also have to pay two bucks extra a week."

Albin wondered who could be visiting him. He opened the door and there was his sister, Olga, and brother, August. They grabbed him and hugged him and everybody started talking at once.

"Wait!" said Albin. "How did you find me?"

"We knew you were coming to Chicago so we just got off the train and started asking around if anyone had seen a short Finn who liked to wrestle," August said. "Seems like everybody in town knows ya."

"A fella named Clancy told us where to find you and your landlady let us in when I said you was my brother."

Then Olga broke the bad news to Albin: Hilda got engaged to a fellow when she never heard from you.

Albin was shocked.

"But how can that be! I wrote to Hilda every day, except when I was on freight train coming here, and when I was on a ship to Portland, and when I was at Sointula where they didn't have regular mail pick up…"

Olga said, "I don't know, Albin. If your letters

were going to her house then maybe her brother was putting them away so she couldn't see them. You know he never liked you."

It all began to come clear to Albin. This was why he never got a letter from Hilda. "She didn't get mine so she didn't know where to send hers." Albin began to pace the floor. He was so distraught his brother stopped him and made him sit down.

"Albin, you need to calm down. I don't think they are married yet so there is still time. You must write a letter to Hilda's brother and tell him to ask Hilda to wait. You must also tell him to give her the letters if he still has them."

Albin thought about what August said. "It may work," he told August, "but then what if Hilda has fallen in love with this man? I wouldn't stand in her way if she doesn't love me anymore. After all, what do I have to offer her? Life in an unfamiliar place. No money to get a house. I don't even have a decent job yet," he lamented.

Olga said, "Listen to August, Albin. Do what he says and maybe you will be pleasantly surprised. There's always hope."

So once more Albin sat down to write a letter,

this time to Hilda's brother, John.

* * *

A month-long round of engagement parties took place at the Guddals' home. Many of their friends had parties as well, all to honor the bride and groom. Horseback riding parties were held almost every weekend, and a cruise on a friend's big yacht in the Gulf of Bothnia between Sweden and Finland was a wonderful surprise.

Hilda had never been on a large yacht before. She was amazed at the luxury aboard the vessel and all of the staterooms for guests, which included both sets of parents, some of their friends and a few elderly relatives, and friends of both Sven and Hilda.

Wonderful banquets were prepared throughout the days and nights, and a ballroom for dancing to a small band was especially popular for the young people. They also had a sauna on board which was popular with young and old alike.

Hilda began sewing on her wedding gown the day after they returned from the cruise. This was the dress in which she had planned to be married to Albin. She had purchased the white satin and the tulle for the veil shortly after Albin had left for

America. Now that Albin was gone from her life she would wear the gown for her marriage to Sven, which was now just two weeks away.

On the eve of the wedding, Hilda had been in tears for two days. She didn't want to marry Sven. She went to his house to tell him, but he wasn't home. His mother asked her to come in. She could tell how upset Hilda was.

Hilda spilled her heart out to Marta Guddal. She told her about Albin and even though she hadn't heard from him, she was still in love with him, and he with her — she could feel it.

"Sven is a very nice boy, Mrs. Guddal. I know he will find a lovely woman to be his wife. But I can't marry him when I have these feelings for my Albin," Hilda cried.

Marta put her arms around Hilda and said, "I understand, Hilda my dear. I would have liked nothing better than to have you for a daughter-in-law, but if you are in love with another man, both of you would be miserable in a marriage that wasn't meant to be.

"Go to America, child. Go find your Albin. I'm sure he must be waiting for you there."

Hilda thanked this wonderful and loving woman. She kissed Marta and said, "You are a very gracious lady and I shall never forget you. Thank you for all you have done for me."

Hilda ran all the way home to John's house and went straight to the library where she found him and Mary sitting at a table talking about the wedding, she supposed.

"Forget it Mary, John — there's not going to be any wedding. Not to Sven, anyway," Hilda blurted out.

"I just came from Sven's house and told his mother I couldn't marry her son because I am in love with Albin. She will have to break the news to him....

I can't."

Mary took Hilda in her arms and said, "John has done a terrible thing, dear Hilda." She turned to John and said, "Give Hilda the letters."

John had a large package in his hands. He said, "Before I do, Hilda, there's something you should know.

"I was only thinking of your welfare when I hid Albin's letters."

Hilda let out a gasp. "You—you have letters from Albin? Oh, John, how long have you had them?"

She began to cry. When he handed her the letters he tried one last time to try to convince Hilda he really thought keeping them from her was a good thing. Hilda wasn't buying it. She grabbed the letters and fled to her room.

Hilda lay on her bed with the many letters spread out. She picked up the one with the earliest postmark and began to read. Three hours went by and it began to get dark, making it difficult to see Albin's writing through her tears.

Exhausted just from the emotion of going through most of Albin's letters in a few hours, Hilda went downstairs and into the kitchen where Mary was preparing supper. She went to John and slipped her arms around his neck.

"I forgive you, John. I know you did what you thought was best for me. You weren't certain that Albin and I could make it in America. And you may be right. It may not be a perfect life over there.

"From the way Albin writes in his letters, life is pretty hard."

"Yes, Hilda," John said. "And I'm really sorry for deceiving you. I will try to make it up to you.

"In the morning, we will go to the bank and I will draw enough out for you and Albin to get a decent start in your marriage in America." Hilda thought she saw John brush away a tear from his cheek. That would be a first, she thought.

She gave her brother a squeeze and went over to help Mary with supper.

John watched Hilda put on an apron and thought: "I don't think I can tolerate burnt biscuits tonight!"

John said, "You don't need to help with supper, Hilda. Save your cooking skills for your new husband!"

They all laughed at John's joke about Hilda's "cooking skills".

Hilda went back to her room and wrote a letter to Albin and checked to see where his latest letter was posted. "Chicago, eh? He made it to the big city after all...where all the women are!"Hilda spent two days packing for her trip to America. John purchased a large trunk for her. Most of her clothes would fit in that. Several small suitcases were packed with sewing material and notions, favorite books, and also some of the gifts she received for what was to be for her wedding to Sven. "Might as well take them along. I won't know anyone in America to give me wedding presents. I'm sure Sven and his mother won't mind."

And so a lot of new things for beginning a household were packed along in Hilda's luggage and the big steamer trunk.

She was so busy making out lists of what she needed to remember she almost didn't hear the knock on her door. "Come in," said Hilda, thinking it was Mary.

Tarja Paavinen came in with her children, Martin and little Esteri. She had quit her job as nanny for Tarja when she began making wedding plans so she hadn't seen them for several weeks.

She hugged Tarja and then pulled Martin and Esteri onto her lap. "Oh, I'm going to miss you all so much. Maybe some day you can come visit me in America."

Tarja said, "Maybe that day is sooner than you think. There is much uncertainty of what is happening in Finland now, and I just got a large bonus from your brother with a note that said it was owed to me after my husband's death. With the money I have saved, I have enough for our passage!"

"Oh, Tarja!" Hilda said. Maybe we can sail on the same ship. You would be a great help to me as well as companionship on the trip, and I could take care of these wonderful darlings for you.

"I would so like you to sail with me," and she hugged the children again.

Hilda and Tarja decided to go to the steamship company the next day and book their passage. They would all be starting a new life in a new country!

ALBIN'S LETTERS

Chapter 19

August and Olga found a flat with two
bedrooms near downtown Chicago. They moved
in and began to make plans for Albin and Hilda's
wedding.

Albin had just received a letter from Hilda
telling him the wedding to the Swede was off, and
she had gotten all of his letters in one big package.

He would be at the train station when she
arrived and take her to his rooming house. Maybe
Liz would find them larger quarters.

The big ship gave a lurch and startled Hilda out
of a deep sleep. She had been having this strange
dream and both Albin and Sven were in it. She
tried to remember the sequence of events in the
dream but all she could recall was the two men in
her life arguing with one another. Superstitious as
Hilda was, she didn't give any real credence to the
dream and blamed it on the huge meal served the

night before in the ship's dining room. The huge slice of apple pie with ice cream on top and the wonderful strong Swedish-style coffee completed the sumptuous meal, topped off with coffee laced with whiskey, saucered and sipped through a sugar lump. Hilda's last recollection was being helped to her stateroom by the cabin steward when he found her leaning over the ship's rail.

She looked out the porthole and saw that the ship had docked and the morning sun was coming up over the Atlantic Ocean, and realized she was finally on the last leg of her long journey to meet Albin.

She began to gather her belongings when she heard the loud announcement by the ship's stewards throughout the ship: "All ashore that's going ashore!"

The End

EPILOGUE

Hilda arrived in Chicago on the train a day earlier than she expected, so Albin wasn't there to greet her. She hired a horse-drawn cab to take her to the north side apartment. When Hilda got there, they talked to Ida (Hilda's sister, who had moved to Chicago years earlier and married a man named Finnstrom) who had heard about the place where Albin was staying. Hilda went straight to the address of Albin's building and knocked on the door. When Liz opened the door, she looked at the well-groomed young Hilda and said, "Yer must be Albin's lady friend."

"Indeed I am. Please direct me to Albin's room."

She went to the door and found it open. There was Albin, drinking from a pail of beer and talking to a young woman.

"Oh, Hilda! You weren't supposed to be here until tomorrow!"

"I wanted to surprise you. I guess I did," Hilda

said and looked at the young woman.

"Oh, Hilda, this is a friend, Stephanie. She lives in one of the other rooms."

Stephanie mumbled a hello and went out the door.

"I hope I didn't scare her away," Hilda said and sniffed the air. "What is that smell?"

"You will get used to it," Albin said. "No, I won't," countered Hilda.

He approached her and said, "C'mon, Hilda, don't I even get a little kiss?"

"Yes, Albin, but I want you to get your things together right now. I want you to move in with me at Ida's. You aren't going to live in this…this… boarding house another minute."

And then she grabbed Albin and kissed him full on the mouth.

So the loving reunion between Hilda and Albin set the tone for their married life, which was to begin very soon.

But first they had to get married. Albin didn't have enough money to buy a suit for the wedding, or wedding rings, or to pay the minister. Hilda, with her brother John's help, took care of it all. They spent their honeymoon at Ida's, playing with Martin and Esteri. Hilda learned how to cook in an American kitchen, but burned the porridge anyway. Albin found a job making copper pipes which were all the rage with so much plumbing beginning to move inside the houses. Indoor plumbing for the kitchen sinks came to the big cities first. Toilets had to wait awhile.

Albin wrestled in contests with his brother, August, and the two enjoyed some degree of fame. Hilda and Albin's first baby came along a year later. They named her Esteri. She would be followed by four brothers.

✳✳✳

Albin's Letters

Recipes

Following are some Swedish and Finnish Recipes Hilda never made, or ruined if she did try to make them!

Swedish Meat Balls
(Kottbullar)

2 cups soft bread crumbs	$^1/_2$ tsp pepper
(about 3 slices of day old bread)	1 tsp paprika
$^2/_3$ cups milk	1 tbsp beef bouillon
$^1/_2$ cup minced onion	3 tbsp flour
4 tbsp butter	1 cup water
1 $^1/_2$ lbs. ground beef	a few grains of pepper
3 eggs, slightly beaten	1 cup sour cream
2 tsp salt	2 tbsp minced parsley

Finely dice the onion and sauté gently in a little butter without browning.

Soak the bread crumbs in milk.

Blend the ground meat, preferably in a food processor, with the onion, eggs, milk/bread crumb mixture, bouillon, and spices until well blended.

Add a little water if the mixture feels too firm.

Scoop meat mixture with a teaspoon and shape into

1-inch balls. In a skillet over medium heat, brown a generous pat of butter until it "goes quiet", then place the meatballs in the pan and let them brown on all sides. Shake the frying pan often. When meatballs are done, remove from the pan to a warm plate and keep warm.

Sauté the flour in the pan drippings until toasted. Whisk in 1 cup water and cook and stir a few more minutes until mixture thickens. Turn off the heat, stir in sour cream and parsley, and season with salt and pepper.

Ladle sauce over meatballs and serve with whipped potatoes or soft egg noodles.

Serve with potato purée or boiled potatoes and chilled lingonberry sauce.

Swedish Apple Cake
(Appelkaka)

1 tbsp butter
1 ½ cups thinly sliced apples
⅓ cup firmly packed light brown sugar
1 egg
⅓ cup sugar
½ cup sifted all-purpose flour
1 tsp double action baking powder
¼ cup milk
whipped cream

Spread butter over bottom of an 8-inch layer cake pan. Mix apples and brown sugar and spread evenly in pan.

Beat egg until light; beat in sugar. Sift together flour and baking powder and add to egg mixture alternately with milk.

Pour batter over apples in pan. Bake in moderate oven (350°F) for 30 to 35 minutes.

Turn out upside down on cake plate. Serve warm with whipped cream.

Chicken Sibelius

2 whole chicken breasts, boned & cut into 3 inch pieces
1 tsp salt
$^1/_8$ tsp poultry seasoning
¼ cup butter or margarine
2 - 10 oz. pkgs. frozen asparagus, cooked & drained
1 - 10 oz. can condensed cream of chicken soup
½ cup light cream
½ tsp curry powder
1 cup Finnish Swiss cheese

Season chicken with salt and poultry seasoning. Melt butter in large skillet, and sauté chicken until lightly browned. Arrange asparagus in bottom of greased 1½ quart shallow baking dish. Top with chicken. Combine soup, cream and curry powder. Pour over chicken and asparagus. Top with cheese. Bake uncovered at 350°F for 30 minutes, or until chicken is tender. Serves 4.

Finnish Oven Cakes

(From *The Atkinson Family Cookbook* by Rosie Atkinson;
Recipe by Brent Wofford)

4 eggs
2 tbs sugar
2 cups milk
1 cup flour
¼ cup melted butter

Beat eggs.
Add rest of ingredients and beat together.
Bake in 9" x 12" greased pan at 400°F For 30 minutes.
Serve with sugar, syrup or fresh berries.

Finnish Sour Cream Rings
(From *The Atkinson Family Cookbook* by Rosie Atkinson;
Recipe by Sue Neher)

1 cup butter
1 cup sugar
½ cup sour cream
½ tsp salt
1 tsp almond flavoring
3 cups flour

Cream butter. Gradually add sugar, blending thoroughly. Add remaining ingredients; chill. Roll piece of dough into long pencil thick rolls. Cut into 4-inch lengths. Bring ends together slightly overlapping; dip in additional sugar. Place on greased cookie sheet. Bake at 400°F for 10-12 minutes. Makes 7 dozen.

Finnish Whipped Berry Pudding
(Vispi Puuro)
(From *The Atkinson Family Cookbook* by Rosie Atkinson;
Recipe by Linda Gilje)

2 cups berries, any kind
4 cups water
1 cup sugar
¾ cups farina

Boil berries in water until soft. Puree the juice
and berries through strainer. Add sugar, bring t
boil. Gradually add farina, stirring constantly. Let
mixture simmer on low heat until farina thickens,
then remove.

Whip the pudding until it becomes fluffy and cool.
Pour into serving bowl. Serve with rich cream
or milk.

Finnish Almond Sticks

(From *The Atkinson Family Cookbook* by Rosie Atkinson;
Recipe by Sue Neher)

2 ½ cups flour
½ cup sugar
1 tsp almond extract
1 cup butter
1 beaten egg
¼ cup sugar
1 cup finely chopped blanched almonds

Mix flour, sugar and flavoring. Cut in butter. Press together to form dough and chill. Divide into 8 pieces. Roll each piece into a long roll about finger thickness.

Place rolls of dough next to each other. Brush beaten egg on top of the rolls. Sprinkle with sugar and almonds. Cut into 2-inch lengths. Bake on grease sheets at 350°F for 15 minutes. About 6 dozen.

ACKNOWLEDGEMENTS

FINE FINNISH FOODS
Collected by Gerry Kangas and Finns for Progress
Copyright 1988 by Penfield Press, 215 Brown Street, Iowa City IA 52245. Julin Printing Company.

THE ATKINSON FAMILY COOKBOOK
A collection of recipes from the author's husband's family, one of whom was married to a Finn named Eero Waali.
Copyright 1992 by Rosie Atkinson, published in Bremerton, Washington

SWEDISH RECIPES, OLD & NEW
Copyright 1955 by American Daughters of Sweden, Chicago, Illinois, December, 1955

RAINCOAST CHRONICLES
Copyright Canada 1976 Harbour Publishing, Madeira Park, British Columbia

ELLIS ISLAND ARCHIVES
www.ellisislandrecords.com

ALBIN'S LETTERS

About the Author

Rosie was born in Chicago, Illinois, and showed an early interest in writing and art. She wrote poetry as a young homemaker and took drawing classes at her local community college.

After fourteen years in the newspaper business, first as columnist for *The Port Orchard Independent*, and then as Women's Editor at *The Bremerton Sun*, she retired and her focus turned to writing fiction. She then joined Peninsula Chapter, Romance Writers of America.

Cruising the waters of Puget Sound and Canadian waters with her husband Charlie and 6 children in the family boat, Puget Rose, gave rise to many articles published in *Nor'westing*, *Sea* and other regional boating magazines. She also wrote a column for a weekly Kitsap County publication, *Wednesday Magazine*.

She still writes on a daily basis and is a member of Washington and National Federation of Press Women.

Made in the USA
Charleston, SC
10 August 2013